I0847319

Sweet Redemption

HONEYSUCKLE TEXAS ★ BOOK 7

CHRIS KENISTON

Indie House Publishing

Indie House Publishing

CHAPTER ONE

"*Are we really going to do this again?*" *Clint took a deep breath and clamping his eyes shut, counted to five before exhaling. It was getting harder and harder to communicate with Carol. He'd tried his best, working two jobs, moving them to a larger house in a nicer neighborhood, holding his old blue Ford together with spit and a prayer instead of getting a new work truck the way he needed.*

He just didn't understand what had gone so wrong. Why was his wife so terribly miserable? Happy one day, desperate the next. He'd begged her to go to therapy; even though he couldn't afford it, he'd find a way. Something had to give. With Jason tucked in and sound asleep, he started for the kitchen to help clean up after their dinner of warmed up canned ravioli, only to have Carol start throwing silverware at him. Instead of reasoning with her, he gave up. Grabbed his jacket and his keys and headed for Kelsey's bar. He'd probably had one, okay, two more than he should have, and he probably shouldn't have gotten behind the wheel of his truck, but he needed to escape from the hell his marriage had become at least for a few hours.

Parking in the driveway, he almost tripped into the house, collapsing on the lumpy sofa rather than make his way upstairs and risk another fight with Carol. He'd been asleep before he remembered closing his eyes.

Hot. Fan, he needed the fan. So hot. No. November. Not hot. No fan. Rolling slightly, he almost slid off the sofa. That's right. Not in bed. So hot. Blinking, he looked for the fan, but couldn't see. Blinked again. And again. Still so dark. Then he heard it. A sizzle, or a crackle, or... his eyes flew open. Fire. The house was on fire. The kitchen was bright orange. The dining room sparked. The stairs. He needed to get to the stairs. His lungs felt weighted. Heavy. Hard. Pulling the hem of his shirt up over his nose and mouth with one arm, he stumbled to his feet. Had to get upstairs. So much smoke. Something somewhere in the back of his mind repeated, stop, drop, and roll, only he wasn't on fire...yet. Still, he got down on all fours and crawled up the stairs, barely able to make out where he was going. The smoke was so thick. Feeling his way as much as looking, he found Jason's door. Ignoring the sharp pain on the burning knob, he opened the door and hurried inside. On his bed, coughing but asleep, his son was at least still breathing.

Clint threw a blanket over Jason's head, then placing another around them both, upright now, he rushed out the door and down the stairs. The living room was almost fully engulfed. The sofa he'd been sleeping on only minutes ago was a sea of dancing orange and yellow flames, shooting high to the ceiling. He barely had a path to the front door.

Not caring about his hands, he pulled the door open and hurried outside, nearly collapsing on the lawn. Carol. He had to get Carol. Only at that moment, still coughing, Jason hacked out, "Daddy."

"It's okay, Son. You're okay." Turning his head, the house was almost fully engulfed. Windows exploded as flames continued to burst through the house.

"You wait here," he told his son, then turned to the house.

"Clint." A hand clamped on his arm. "You can't go back in there." It was Jerry, their next-door neighbor. "We called the fire department. They're on their way."

"Carol," was all he managed to spit out. "I have to get Carol."

He saw Jerry's eyes widen. The neighbor on his other side had turned on the hose and was watering down his own roof, turning the spout from time to time toward Clint's house.

"It's too dangerous," Jerry repeated, his grip on Clint's arm even tighter. "You can't."

"Carol!" he shouted as loud as he could, as if she could hear him and would wake up and run out of the house on her own two feet. *"Carol!"* he screamed again.

"Clint!" another male voice shouted at him.

"Carol!" He had to save Carol.

"Clint!" the voice shouted louder. "Wake up, man."

Wake up? Clint blinked, forcing his eyelids open. Where was he? The fire. No. Not the fire. Not his house. And then, closing his eyes, he slumped back against his pillow.

"You okay?" The voice belonged to Benny, the new hand they'd hired.

It was all coming back to him. He wasn't living in Wyoming anymore. He was in Texas. Working on the Sweet Ranch. A foreman. If he wasn't so exhausted from his nightmare, he would have laughed at that. "Sorry, kid. I guess it was a bad dream."

"One helluva dream. You were screaming so loud I thought the place was on fire."

Right. On fire. "Sorry." Since they'd fixed up the old foreman's house for one of the Sweet newlyweds, he'd insisted he'd be fine bunking with Benny. Now maybe he should have given that more thought. "I'm okay. You go back to sleep."

Nodding, Benny straightened, eyed him a moment longer, probably convincing himself that Clint was indeed okay, and then turned on his heel and went back to his bunk in the other room.

Unlike most bunkhouses, this one was broken into more private cubicles with a living area in the middle, so he stayed on his end and Benny moved into the other end. Throwing his feet over the side of the bed, he dropped his face into his hands, then wiping the sweat from his forehead, raked his fingers through his hair and blew out a long slow breath. He'd thought the nightmares had finally stopped. Pushing to his feet, he walked to the single photo that had survived that horrible night. Him and Jason in happier days. That sunny-faced little boy brought a smile to his face. What Clint wouldn't give to go back in time and fix everything.

"This is heaven." Alice Sweet sat in a rocker. There was no place on the planet she loved more than the view of the horizon from this porch. The plans she and Kade had worked out for a guest annex would have a nice little porch with the same view over Sweet land under the Texas sky. Someday, when it was time, she'd move out of the big house and into the smaller one. And that would be just fine with her. Until then, though, she had about fifteen more minutes to enjoy her coffee before it was time to head back into the house and deal with her chores. Maybe it was time to add cleaning up the garden to her chore list. Since Charlie passed, she couldn't bring herself to mess with it. For them it hadn't been a chore, it had been something fun they did together, oohing and aahing over flavorful vegetables and laughing when they grew into odd shapes or big enough to make the record books. Maybe.

"Mind a little company?" Her newest daughter-in-law Cassie stood in the doorway.

"Of course not." She patted the arm of the big green rocking chair beside her. "The sky is big enough for everyone."

"That's sort of what I thought the first day I arrived here." Cassie settled into the seat. Rather than kick the chair into motion, she put her feet up on the caned seat and leaned back. "I heard from Jacob's father today."

"Oh," Alice had been very proud of her town, the way everyone came together to help Jacob's family and make sure that Emily got the treatment she needed. There hadn't even been a need for an official fundraiser, folks just came forward and before anyone knew it, everything was arranged and moving forward.

"The judge signed off on the deal. Jacob will have to have scheduled therapy and do community service, but he won't be doing any jail time."

"Oh good." Another reason to smile. The district attorney hadn't been very cooperative at first, but with the whole town, including the bank manager, standing behind Jacob, the guy was left with little choice but to negotiate a deal. Now, things should improve for the family, and that had Alice smiling.

"Is this a private party?" Strolling up the walkway, Rachel had been working in the barn with Clint before her first appointment of the day.

Alice shook her head, then tipped it toward the kitchen door. "Just made a fresh pot."

The two sat in contented silence until Rachel came to sit at her mother's other side. "This is the perfect weather. Cool enough not to sweat, warm enough not to need a jacket. Too bad it only lasts a short while."

"I suspect that's why California became so popular so fast. Mild weather all year long. Not too hot, not too cold." Alice thought back to her one visit with her Charlie to San Francisco and the surrounding coastline. It was their twentieth anniversary. Kade had already signed up for the military and her sister Liz stayed to make sure the younger ones didn't burn the place down. Of course, Jillian, always having been the responsible one, probably could have kept her older brothers in line, but even with a responsible adult in charge, Alice was still just a tad nervous about the homestead in her absence. By the time they were wine tasting in Napa and Sonoma, she wasn't all that worried about the kids back home anymore.

"How come you and Daddy didn't travel more?" Rachel asked over the brim of her mug.

"We talked about it. Came really close to taking a little trip to Mexico. A beach. But why go all the way to another country, that speaks another language, when we can have a view like this any day of the week, including killer sunrises and sunsets."

"I'll second that." Cassie nodded. "The sunsets here are amazing. The stars aren't bad either."

The dark of night under a sea of stars had always been her and Charlie's favorite time of day. Sometimes they'd go sit down by the canyon and put a blanket down to lie on and just enjoy the show.

"I still miss him," Rachel murmured.

Alice nodded. "I know baby." She really missed him too. Some days more than others, especially this last year with all the trouble from Ray and his posse of crooks. The funny thing is, as their family has grown, she didn't miss him quite as much as she once did, and wasn't that something to think about. Another thought struck as she sipped on her lukewarm coffee: when was the last time she'd talked to Charlie?

An engine rumbled loudly from the direction of the front yard and Alice glanced down at her wrist watch. Almost eleven thirty. She should get up and start lunch. It was looking like they were going to have a crowd today.

The back door opened and Carson came onto the porch. "Are men welcome?" he teased.

"Always." Alice smiled at her son.

"I come bearing gifts." He tipped his head toward the kitchen. "Agnes had a couple of leftover tuna casseroles after yesterday's special. She remembered how much you love her tuna casserole so she sent them home with me. You won't have to cook tonight."

"She sure is right about that. I have no idea what she puts in that casserole, but it's almost addictive. It will be a nice treat."

"I have to admit," Rachel set her chair rocking, "everything seems so much brighter now that the ranch isn't at risk anymore."

"It still has a lot of debt," Preston said as he came through the same door.

Alice was going to need to get a bigger back porch.

"We've cleared the delinquent payments, and we've made some changes, gotten some new equipment," Preston smiled momentarily, "but all of it, including the new barns, are going to have to be paid for."

"They will." Alice nodded. Her husband had figured it all out. When he was done with all his expansion plans, the Sweet Ranch would provide for generations to come. He'd be happy to see his brood settled with such perfect soulmates.

"The good news," Preston continued, "is that with the money we'll get from this year's calves, we'll be able to increase the herd. Another year and we will have the four thousand head Dad wanted."

"We'll need more hands." Alice knew that with Kade stepping in for his dad soon, that would be one less man needed, but even before the larger herd, they still had six hands including the foreman. "When do you think we can take on another man?"

Preston looked to his siblings, bypassing his mom. As if she didn't know what they were thinking. The first big trust payment would be coming in a few months. She turned a blind eye to their using the newly married payment to save the ranch, but there was no way she was going to let any of her kids use the money that was meant to help set up their new families, on the ranch. Not on her watch.

CHAPTER TWO

The first pot of coffee had perked and brewed, its rich aroma mingling with the dewy morning. Pouring herself a mug with a dash of milk and sugar, Alice practically inhaled the first sip. She didn't know how anyone could start their day without this delectable, eye-opening brew.

A glance out the kitchen window confirmed what her bones already knew—a dark canvas with the warm glow of a sun that wasn't quite ready to make its morning appearance. When it did, the sun would shine brightly on the Sweet Ranch. Stealing a glimpse at the old clock over the fridge, the time, four forty-five. The family would be stirring soon, needing breakfast before the day's work began. The darkness, the horizon, this kitchen, and her morning ritual, all of it familiar and comforting.

One more sip, one more look into the horizon before she began cracking eggs, and a flicker of motion near the paddocks caught her eye. She squinted, peering through the glass, but the darkness made it hard to distinguish shapes. Could have been Brady on his nightly rounds. Coyotes, maybe, or one of those pesky skunks that had been getting into the trash lately. No rancher let their imagination run amok with boogeymen. She was no different.

She grabbed her favorite heavy sweater from the hook by the back door and slipped outside. The air hit her with a surprising chill, the grass beneath her boots wet with dew. She pulled the sweater tighter around her shoulders, wishing she'd thought to grab a proper coat. In the gray half-light before dawn, shadows took on strange shapes, stretching across the yard toward the barn.

This was no horror movie where the stupid heroine went down into the basement where the axe murderer hid; this was her ranch and she had nothing to fear. Still, she wished she'd thought to grab her gun on the way out the door—just in case.

A crash from the direction of the equipment shed made her jump. Then came a string of colorful curses that definitely weren't coming from any shadow. "Come back here, you little troublemaker!"

Clint? Alice moved toward the voice, curiosity quickening her steps. As she rounded the corner of the barn, her hand flew to her mouth and she stopped in her tracks. Clint, normally so composed and capable, was flat on his backside in the mud, while a small calf pranced just out of his reach. The little thing looked for all the world like it was laughing at him.

"Need a hand?" Alice couldn't keep the amusement from her voice.

Clint's head whipped toward her, surprise flashing across his face. "Mrs. Sweet. I didn't mean to disturb you."

"You didn't. I was just about to start breakfast."

The calf, taking advantage of Clint's distraction, darted behind the water trough.

With a muttered curse that cut off abruptly, Clint scrambled to his feet. "Little escape artist got out of the pen somehow." Wiping his muddy hands on his equally muddy jeans, he shook his head. "Mama's raising a ruckus in the barn, and I'd rather not wake the whole county."

As if on cue, an angry bellow echoed from inside the barn. The calf's head popped up, ears perked, before it took off again.

"Well, we can't have that." Alice pushed her sleeves up her forearms. "I'll circle around the other side. We can herd it back together."

Clint looked like he might object, but another crash had him nodding in agreement. "Just be careful. Ground's slick."

They split up, Clint heading left and Alice circled wide to come around from the other direction. The sky was lightening now, the first hints of pink and gold touching the horizon, giving her just enough light to see by. The calf emerged from behind the shed, spotted her, and changed direction. That little stinker was small but surprisingly quick, darting around with the agility of something much less clumsy-looking.

"This way!" she called to Clint, who was now behind the calf, trying to drive it toward the barn. "If we can get it to the paddock gate…" Her words cut off as the calf made a sudden, sharp turn, heading straight for her. Instinctively, she spread her arms wide, making herself bigger. "Whoa, little one!"

The calf skidded to a halt, looking confused. For a moment, they stared at each other, Alice and this small, stubborn creature caught in a silent standoff. Then, from behind the calf, Clint lunged. Everything happened at once. The calf bolted sideways. Clint's momentum carried him forward, straight toward Alice. She stepped back reflexively, her heel hitting a patch of slick mud. Her feet went out from under her. Arms windmilling, she felt herself falling. A strong hand grabbed for her, catching her arm.

Startled by the commotion, the calf took off across the yard. From the barn came the mother cow's frantic bellow, louder now, more insistent.

"Oh, crud. If it makes it to the main gate, it might get hurt trying to cross the cattle grids."

Clint nodded, and as if the dang animal could understand English, it circled around and began rushing in the opposite direction.

"At this rate," Alice heaved a sigh as she started running, "we could be at this all day!"

The chase was on again, the two of them circling wide, trying to flank the small black-and-white blur that darted back and forth across the yard with the energy only a young animal possesses.

As the morning light strengthened, Alice caught glimpses of Clint's face—focused, determined. Thank heaven for their new foreman. Now if they could just nab the blasted calf.

This blasted calf was going to be the death of him. Clint cut across the yard at a diagonal, boots digging into the wet earth, trying to head off the small blur that was currently making a beeline for the south pasture. For such a small creature, it moved with incredible speed and agility, darting left when he went right, feinting one way before breaking in another direction entirely.

Near him, Alice Sweet kept the pace, her breath coming in quick puffs of white in the cold morning air. This wasn't the first time he'd seen her working the ranch—hard, and yet, with mud splattered up the legs of her jeans and determination etched into every line of her face, he was struck by the strength of the family matriarch.

"We need to cut it off before it escapes again!" She changed direction to circle wide around the water trough.

Clint nodded, adjusting his own trajectory. The sky was lightening rapidly now. If they didn't catch this little troublemaker soon, the whole household would be up and witness to their ridiculous chase. The thought of the Sweet siblings seeing their dignified mother covered in mud and running after a calf was almost enough to make him smile. Almost.

The calf skidded around the corner of the equipment shed, hooves kicking up divots of wet earth. It spotted Alice coming from the left and veered sharply right—straight toward Clint.

"I've got him!" Clint dived forward. His fingers grazed the calf's hide before the little escape artist spun away, bleating what sounded suspiciously like laughter. Clint landed hard on his knees, mud splattering up his already-filthy jeans. "Son of a—" He bit off the curse, remembering who was with him.

"I've heard worse." Alice hurried past, surprisingly spry for a woman wrestling mud that gripped at your boots like suction cups and a calf that might just outwit them both.

The calf made a break for the open space between the

barn and the corral. From inside the barn, the mother cow's bellows were reaching a fever pitch, echoing across the yard. He had no clue how the young calf had managed to escape and not the mama.

"We need to work together," Alice called, circling back. "Drive him toward the barn door. I'll block the exit if he tries to bolt."

Clint nodded, pushing himself up. They moved in tandem, Clint herding from behind while Alice positioned herself to block potential escape paths. The calf darted one way, then another, finding itself increasingly boxed in. Its movements grew more frantic, less coordinated.

"Easy now," Alice murmured, her voice suddenly gentle. "Easy, little one. Your mama's waiting."

The calf slowed, seeming to respond to her tone. Its head turned toward the barn, ears perked at the sound of its mother's calls.

"That's it." Alice took a slow step forward. "Just a little closer…"

The moment shattered as the calf spooked, bolting straight at Clint with the speed and determination of something three times its size. He braced himself, arms spread wide, ready to make the catch—and slipped. His boot heel shot out from under him on the mud-slicked ground, arms flailing as he fought for balance. This was insane. How could one little calf turn two seasoned ranchers into a routine worthy of the Keystone Cops?

Again the mother cow called and the calf flicked an ear toward the bawl, then bolted along the fence line—toward the alley this time.

"That's you!" Clint shouted.

Alice moved like she'd been born in a barn. The calf checked, swung, and there it was, lined up on the run that led straight to the barn door.

"Go," Alice breathed.

They went.

Clint kept pressure steady, not crowding, eyes on hips, not head. If you moved the hip, the front end followed. The calf zigged once more at the broken pallet by the wall, found nowhere to go, and took the center like it was his idea.

"Door?" Alice asked.

"Leave it open." He stole a glance in her direction. "We'll close behind."

Frantic to find her calf, the mama's bawl rolled over them, even louder now, and the calf answered with a thin, ridiculous sound.

Clint opened his palm to wave at the confused calf and the animal hurried down the center aisle toward the sound that belonged to it.

"Stall three." He pointed. "If she's in there—"

"She is." Alice nodded. "Boots is on four. We moved the pair last night."

He liked that she knew where every animal slept without checking a board.

The cow threw her head when she saw them, whites showing, big body swinging to guard the stall door, then swung again when her nose caught the calf. A different sound came out of her, relief and irritation braided together. Alice was already at the latch, fingers quick. "On your count."

"Now."

He slid, she pulled, and the door eased open just enough to let a calf through and not a freight train of a worried mama. The calf shot inside. The cow dropped her head, checked the baby like she was counting toes, then bumped it toward the udder with all the softness a thirteen-hundred-pound animal could manage. The calf latched. The cow blew. Horses shifted in their stalls. Only then did he let his shoulders fall.

"You okay?" Her voice was low enough not to rile the cow.

He nodded. His lungs were still dragging at the air like it was heavy. Sweat cooled at the base of his neck. "He's got legs."

"He's got opinions." The corners of her mouth lifted in a smile. "We should name him Houdini."

The cow lifted her head and huffed at them. Alice

huffed back, softer. "We're going," she told the cow.

They stepped back from the stall in unison. Backs against the wooden walls, each heaved a relieved sigh. Slowly, Alice slid to the ground, her legs stretched out.

Clint slid to sit beside her. His head resting back against the wall, he shook his head. "I don't think I've worked that hard in years."

"Tell me about it." Her shoulders began to shake and for a moment, he thought she was crying. Then he heard it—laughter. Not the polite chuckle he'd occasionally heard from her over the last several months, but full-bodied, unrestrained laughter that seemed to bubble up from someplace deep and genuine. "The look on your face," she gasped between fits of giggles, pushing herself up slightly to look at him. There was mud on her cheek, in her hair, and her eyes were bright with tears of mirth. "When that calf charged you…"

Suddenly, inexplicably, Clint was laughing too. The absurdity of it all—the dignified foreman and the ranch matriarch sprawled in the mud, outwitted by thirty pounds of stubborn calf—struck him full force. The laughter felt rusty, unfamiliar, but it came anyway, rumbling up from a place he'd thought long since gone quiet.

CHAPTER THREE

"**M**orning, Mooooom." Carson stopped in his tracks as Alice slowly made her way from the stove to the table. "What's wrong?"

"Nothing a long soak in a very hot tub won't solve." She'd hoped she'd be done with preparing breakfast before anyone came downstairs. The moment she'd returned to the house, she'd stripped out of her very muddy clothes, hopped into the longest hot shower she dared take and still get breakfast on the table, and then with every move she made, the aches in her sore muscles seemed to escalate exponentially. She hurt in places she'd forgotten she had muscles.

"Beg your pardon?" Carson stood, rooted to the floor, staring at his mother.

On a heavy sigh, she set the platter of bacon down in the middle of the table and slowly turned to face him. "I had a little work out thanks to the new calf. It escaped the barn and Clint and I did a little Three Stooges routine trying to catch him. If we keep that calf, its name will be Houdini. Best escape artist I've ever seen."

To her surprise, rather than be upset, or all protective, Carson bit back a laugh.

"What is so funny?"

Shaking his head and taking a seat, he raised his open palmed hand to his mother. "Sorry. But honestly, I'd have paid big bucks to see that. How's Clint doing?"

"Fine, I'm sure."

Giggling as they came down the stairs, Jess and Cassie entered the kitchen.

"Morning." Jess made a beeline for the coffee pot,

barely slowing to brush her hand across her husband's back before arriving at her destination.

Standing by the table, Cassie sniffed the air like a bloodhound on the hunt. "This kitchen always smells so amazing first thing in the morning."

"Everything's ready." Alice bit down hard on her back teeth as she stretched to reach for the plates in the cabinet. Her shoulder protested the movement with a sharp twinge.

"Mom's had quite the morning already." Carson jumped up from his seat at the table, grabbing the stack of dishes for his mom. "You sit, we've got this."

"If I sit, I'll just hurt more."

"Hurt?" Jess spun around from the sink.

Cassie froze by the tea kettle. "You're hurt?"

"Apparently," Carson set the plates down on the table, "she and Clint were wrangling an escape artist calf."

"Is that a thing?" Cassie looked thoroughly confused.

"No, dear." Alice couldn't help but smile. She really loved that each of her children had found perfect-for-them spouses. Cassie fit in perfectly with ranch life, but the poor kid still had a lot to learn. "Most calves stick close to mama."

"When did this happen?" Jess's eyebrows shot up as she poured herself a cup of coffee.

"This morning." Not wanting to stiffen up by sitting still, she reached into the fridge and pulled out the juice she'd squeezed the night before.

"Morning." Jess looked up at the clock. "It's only six thirty now. What the hell were you doing out there before the crack of dawn, but more importantly, what possessed you to chase after cows?"

"Not cows, one cow and it was a calf. Who knew it had better moves than Mohammed Ali?" This was the reaction she would have expected from her sons, not the women in the family.

Carson shrugged, the smile still tugging at his cheeks. "That certainly would explain why you look like you went ten rounds."

"I do not." She might be a little stiff but there wasn't a

single bruise on her. At least not visible to her family.

The back door opened, a thin ribbon of morning air slipping inside. Clint stepped in, hat in hand. He paused at the threshold. He looked every bit as stiff and sore as she felt, though he was making a valiant effort to hide it. His movements were measured, careful, betraying the strain in his muscles.

"Morning." He nodded to the table at large. "Mrs. Sweet, I found how that calf got out."

"Good." She pulled another mug out from the cupboard. "How'd the little devil do it?"

"Loose board on the back of the stall. Mama was too big to fit through, but the little one slipped right out."

One of the many reasons her husband had gone so deep in debt to handle an overload of deferred maintenance.

"I fixed it up for now. Will get some lumber from town later today and do the job right."

"I can help." Carson looked up from his breakfast.

Clint rotated the hat in his hands. "It's really not a two-man job."

"If you're sure?" Carson asked.

"Completely." Clint nodded.

Alice handed him the mug and slowly moved to the table herself, trying her best not to look like a decrepit old woman. "Might as well join us. If anyone deserves a hearty breakfast this morning, it's you." Slower than she would have liked, she gingerly descended into her seat.

"No, thank you. I've got chores to do before I head into town."

She should probably insist he take the day off, but she knew better than anyone that ranches didn't take a holiday because the folks working it had an ache or pain. She was, however, still the official owner of this ranch and she was perfectly willing to throw her weight around. "Who's the boss here?"

His brows buckled and confusion made itself at home in his eyes. "Uh, you are, ma'am."

"We agree on that." She tipped her chin at the empty chair near the heat. "Sit."

For a few seconds, Clint considered refusing again, but good sense kicked in. No point in ticking off the best employer he ever had. Taking a moment to hang his hat on the hook by the door, he crossed to the table and lowered himself into the chair with the careful movements of a man trying not to show pain.

Carson reached for his own cup of coffee. "Sounds like you two had quite the adventure this morning."

"Definitely not business as usual." Clint accepted the plate Cassie passed him with a nod of thanks.

"Mom said y'all were doing a Three Stooges routine." Carson grinned.

"Your mother's being generous. I'd say it was more like the Keystone Cops."

"I have to admit," Jessie took a seat by her husband, "I wish I could have been there to see it."

"Me too," Cassie added. "Too bad we don't have surveillance cameras around here."

Alice Sweet rolled her eyes. "Thank God for small favors."

Her children snickered, and spent the next few minutes gently teasing the family matriarch.

"Just remember," Alice waved a finger at her son, "I'm not the only Sweet family member to slip in the mud while chasing a calf," her gaze narrowed at her son, "or a mutton."

As if told this would be his last meal, Carson swallowed hard and shoveled the rest of his breakfast down at lightning speed.

A satisfied smirk, not a smile, a full-blown smirk, made itself at home on Alice Sweet's face. Clint was going to have to remember to ask her one day, what was the story with Carson and the mutton, since it was pretty obvious to any fool that he did not want his mother sharing that little episode in his life with everyone at the table. Probably, most especially, his new wife.

By the time the morning conversations had come to an

end and the family were gathering their plates and standing, Clint realized he'd scarfed down not one but two plates of the best breakfast he'd had in a very long time. Pushing to his feet, he gathered his plate and empty juice glass.

"I'll take that." Already on her feet, Alice took his dirty dishes. "Give me two minutes to change my shoes and we'll head to town."

"Town?"

Dishes in her hand, she looked up at him, her brows arching high on her forehead. "Where else are we going to buy lumber?"

"It's only a few boards. I can do that on my own. I was planning a trip to town today anyhow to pick up a new auger bit. We seem to be breaking through those at a faster than ever speed lately."

The way Alice Sweet studied him, he wished he could read minds. He didn't have a clue if he'd said something wrong or if she was merely mentally putting together her next grocery list. Another moment and she shook her head. "Have you always been this difficult?"

He knew his eyes must have popped wide as a saucer.

"First I have to practically threaten you to sit down and eat, and now I'm not allowed to go into town to buy my own supplies."

If it were at all possible for his eyes to grow any rounder or perhaps even fall out of his head, they probably would. What had he done? "Uh, I, uh…"

In that split second, a wide smile spread across her face as she continued shaking her head. "As much as I'd love to soak in a hot tub for a week or two, I have things to pick up in town as well, so lose the startled owl look and let's get going."

"Yes, ma'am." There was no way he was putting up a fuss. If she wanted to go to town, the lady was going with him to town. Not till he heard her chuckling as she walked to the back door to change out of her boots, did he fully relax. The last thing he needed was to lose this job. Not with his record.

Clint shifted the truck into drive when the sound hit—

high-pitched whine that morphed into a grinding squeal. Not good.

From the passenger seat, he heard Alice wince. "That doesn't sound healthy."

"No, ma'am." He shifted back to park, cut the engine. "I'd better take a look."

By a heartbeat, Alice beat him to the front of the truck. On her tippy toes, with the practiced ease of someone who had done this before, she was under the hood, scanning for the source of the horrid sound. Her hand moving from one spot to the other, he got the distinct impression that this woman had been under more metal than most men. She made a strangled sound that sounded an awful lot like a growl. "These blasted electronic engines. Give me the old days when all you needed to keep a truck running was a wrench and some baling wire."

Clint couldn't help but smile at that. "Simpler times."

She eased back onto her heels and brushed her hands free of engine grime. "Got any ideas?"

He leaned in closer, listening to the faint tick of cooling metal. "Could be the serpentine belt. Or maybe the alternator." He reached in, fingers tracing the path of the serpentine belt. "My money's on this being the problem. Belt's cracked, starting to fray. Probably slipping on the pulley." He slammed the hood shut. "We'd better take another vehicle. I'll pick up a new belt. Fix it after I get to the boards in the barn."

"Okay."

He felt more than saw her gaze on him as he cut the engine and retrieved the keys.

She fell into step beside him as they made their way to the other ranch truck. Hurrying to match his stride, she glanced up at him. "You seem to know an awful lot about an awful lot."

"My mother would say, just enough to get myself into trouble."

"Did you get into a lot of trouble?" Her question was genuine, but her tone was teasing.

He didn't have to look at her to know those deep blue

eyes would be sparkling with humor. "Usual stuff."

"Who taught you to fix cars?"

"That would be my dad."

"And the carpentry?"

"Dad's Brother." He opened the driver's side door and pulled the keys out from under the mat. Before he could consider opening the door for her, she was already climbing into the passenger seat. "Grandpa was an electrician. Growing up, I learned pretty much everything I'd need to know to fix or build a house—or a ranch."

Buckling her seat belt, she leaned against the door. "So how'd you wind up in ranching?"

"That would be Mom's roots. I'd spend every summer at my grandparents' ranch in Wyoming. I guess I loved cows and horses more than hammers and wrenches. According to my mother, I learned to ride before I could walk." The memory was bittersweet. "They died when I was a teenager. Mom sold the ranch."

Lips pressed tightly together, Alice nodded. "That must have been hard on your mom."

"Yes and no. She loved the ranch as much as I did, but she loved Dad more. They were super tight. They…fit. Balanced each other."

That made Alice smile. He liked seeing her smile. It was a nice smile. "Are they still in Wyoming?"

His chest felt suddenly tight. "My parents passed away not long after I went to—" He caught himself, suddenly aware of how close he'd come to revealing too much. "After I left home. Doctor said it was natural causes, that it was more common than you'd think for one partner to go shortly after the other. Especially when they were as close as my parents were."

"I'm sorry." Sympathy, not pity, shone in her eyes.

He had to wonder, would she look at him the same way if she knew what he knew? The only cause for his parents' death was a broken heart. He'd broken their heart.

CHAPTER FOUR

Alice was going to have to learn to slow down. Going over the list of supplies Clint had dictated to her, she'd managed to decipher almost everything on her chicken scratch list. Save one. Tired of squinting at the page as if that was somehow going to make her letters legible, she shoved the list and pen into her pocket and headed out the back door.

At the barn, she found Benny cleaning out the hooves on a mare. "How's it going?"

The kid lifted his face and smiled at her. "Great, Ms. Sweet."

"Clint taking good care of you?" She glanced around.

"Yes, ma'am. Best boss I've ever had."

Considering the kid looked barely old enough to shave, she doubted he'd had that many bosses. "Any idea where he is?"

The kid nodded. "Yes, ma'am. He's in the workroom. Around the corner."

Smiling, she bit back a chuckle. As if she needed to be told where the work room was. "Thanks."

The door stood half-open. First thing she spotted was the sawhorses, then two boards leaning against the wall, and finally, Clint, focused on another piece of wood in his hands. "Waiting for it to talk back?"

Slowly turning his head to face her, his expression barely shifted, only a hint of a smile teased at one corner of his mouth. "Could be." Now his eyes were twinkling with mirth. It wasn't often she'd catch this serious man smiling, and here twice in just a few days.

Looking more closely at the wooden board he held in

his hands, she inched closer. "Those are our corn hole boards."

"Yes, ma'am."

"I thought they'd been tossed."

"Cleaning out the closet in the tack room, I found these in the back corner. They looked to have been made with love, but seen better days."

Her cheeks pulled at the corner of her mouth. "Charlie made those with the boys a few hundred years ago." She ran her fingers over the one board. "I think the hinges finally gave out."

He bobbed his head. "Figured I'd restore them. Not sure if I can save the artwork."

"It would be nice, but life moves on. We could have Mason help Carson with the artwork."

"Carry on the tradition." Clint's smile widened. It made his eyes sparkle. Nice eyes, the color of warm honey.

He switched paper—120 to 220—and kept his pressure even. No showing off. Just the kind of patient motion that makes things last. The easy movements had her nearly mesmerized. Next, he wiped the board with a tack cloth, a small hiss of dust lifting, then he set the cloth aside and focused on the next board. Always near her now that Kade had reported to his temporary duty, Brady settled at her feet, thumped his tail, and kept the world supervised with eyes mostly closed. She wasn't sure if that counted for approval of the project or not.

So entranced, she'd almost forgotten why she'd come in here. Clearing her throat, she pulled the list from her pocket and stepped closer. "I'm afraid I can't read my own handwriting. Any idea what this line is?"

Setting the newly sanded board to one side, he took the list and perused it from top to bottom. "The hinge pins?"

Her gaze shifted to the list. "Of course. For the broken gates."

"Yes, ma'am." He returned the list.

"Thank you." She turned and for the first time noticed the two finished boards in the corner. "Oh my."

Slowly, she walked over. The boards were beautiful.

Gingerly, almost reverently, she ran her fingers down the edge. Smooth, shiny, and Carson's hand painted flag looked exactly the way she remembered it.

His sanding stopped. "Is that a good 'Oh my' or a bad 'Oh my'?"

"Good." Her head tilted to see him. "It looks even better than the day they finished it. I thought you didn't think you could save the designs?"

He shrugged. "I said maybe. I sanded it just enough to get the old lacquer off, took as little of the paint as I could, then with a little effort here and there, and some touch-up paint there and here…" He shrugged again.

"Don't suppose you found the bags in that mess?"

His chin lifted and tilted to the opposite corner. "In that box over there."

Dragging herself away from the memories of all those years ago, she walked to the box he'd indicated and reached inside. The bags had come from her sister's shop too many years ago. She tossed one in the air ever so slightly, then caught it. Leaning in to grab another, she did the same. They were in pretty good shape. Her hands full, she glanced in Clint's direction. The man had straightened, rolled his shoulders, and was now rolling his neck when the weight of the small bag suddenly felt heavier than it should.

Biting back a smile, she squeezed the one bag, lightly flipped it in her hand, and then, grinning a little wider, leveled her arm in front of her, focused on the mark, and let the beanbag fly.

The handful of beanbags fallen to the floor, Alice Sweet stood across from him, eyes as wide as silver dollars and both hands covering her mouth. Assuming her intent had been to smack him dead center of his chest, the lady had great aim. Good thing it was only a beanbag or he'd be dead where he stood.

Her hands sliding slowly down her face, he could see

her valiant effort not to burst out laughing. "I'm sorry. I don't know what came over me."

"Next time," he bent to scoop the fallen bag, "aim for the board, ma'am. I'm not regulation."

That cost her the laugh she'd desperately tried to withhold. Nearly doubled over with laughter, she finally straightened. "Touché."

It took two long strides to reach her, and return the bag.

Her gaze darted from the bag, to him, to the finished boards across the way. "Are you a betting man?"

He shook his head. "Only on sure things, then it's not gambling."

"Agreed." She nodded and turned on her heel, moved to where the dried boards rested, then spun about to face him. "How about a little friendly competition?"

"Friendly?" The word might mean easygoing and casual, but the glint in her eyes read killer instincts.

Smiling sweetly, too sweetly, she hefted one shoulder in a lazy shrug and then lifted the sack of beanbags out of the box. "Unless you're… chicken?"

"Them's fighting words." He couldn't believe he'd just said that to his boss. "I mean…"

"You're on."

"Excuse me?"

"One match." He lifted the flag board and turned toward the doorway. What was he doing?

Outside, he set the boards up. Walked the distance between the board and where they should stand.

"You've played?" Her one brow arched high over her eye.

"Some."

"Some. Hmm, not sure I like the sound of that." Lining up, she turned to face him. "Want to flip for who goes first?"

He shook his head. "Ladies first." Her entire stance shifted. Concentration ruled. Her one arm swung forward then back, testing, measuring, stalling, he had no idea which was on the mark.

Bobbing her head, it almost looked like she was

communicating with the wooden slab. Her arm lifted, swung back and the bag flew in a perfect arch, landing on the rim of the hole. She tilted sideways, like Don Quixote with the windmills, willing the bag to tip into the hole. When it rested in place, she heaved a sigh and took a step back. "Your turn."

For a short minute, he considered taking it easy on his boss, but that idea disappeared as quickly as it had arrived. Taking a fraction of the time she had, he closed one eye, focused on the board, and then tossed the beanbag with a gentle shove. As Ms. Alice's bag had done, his flew in a perfect arch before sinking in the hole. If it had been a basketball, he would have heard the swoosh. Spinning around, expecting to find his employer annoyed at the ease with which he'd played his turn, he was surprised to see her leaning against the barn, arms and ankles crossed, with sparkling eyes and wide smile.

"You're a ringer. Do my sisters know how good you are? Does anyone?"

All he could do was shake his head. Though he went into town when necessary, a man with his history found that keeping a low profile was best for everyone. "No, ma'am."

She pushed away from the exterior wall and marched with determination to the sack of bags. He'd seen that look before. Alice Sweet was a walking poster child for 'where there's a will there's a way.' Squinting at the board, she dipped her chin, grabbed a bag, and aiming carefully, tossed it across. Again, close but no cigar. "I think what I need is motivation."

Not sure what to say, again, he merely nodded.

Fisting her hands on her hips, she glanced around, pressed her lips tightly together and scanned her surroundings once again. This time her gaze fell toward the back of the house and a sly smile bloomed. "If I win, you have to help clean out that vegetable garden that hasn't been touched since… well, for a couple of years now."

"And if I win?"

She straightened her spine and lifted her chin. "I'll put

in those new fence posts we're needing on that back pasture."

There was no way he was going to let this woman deal with the auger to drill holes for fence posts. That wasn't the best of jobs for one man, never mind one woman. No matter how strong and competent. "I don't…"

He didn't get more than those two words before she held her hand up to him, palm out. "Those are my terms."

His mother would tan his hide if he said yes. On the other hand, he wouldn't put it past Mrs. Sweet to do the same if he said no, or for that matter, if he threw the match. Dang, life really could throw the strangest challenges at a man. "All right." He moved forward and tossed his bags with a little less focus. Even so, three of the four were a hole in one.

Mrs. Sweet was right about at least one thing, motivation did seem to help her game. She landed two out of four.

The next round he succeeded in nailing three out of four again, only this time Mrs. Sweet improved to three out of four as well. He was either going to have to throw the game or let her dig fence post holes. Who knew, at his age, that this would be such a hard choice?

Standing in the same spot he'd stood the last few rounds, he tossed the first two, holes in one, then cringed when not one but two of the next tosses went straight in. There was no way for her to beat him.

Shaking her head, she strode right up to him. No point in throwing since she couldn't beat him. Instead she shoved her hand at him, waiting for him to do the same. When he did, she shook it. Her grip stronger than he'd expected and yet femininely smooth. That oxymoron seemed to fit her perfectly, Strong and smooth. "Looks like you've got yourself a post digger."

"I can't talk you out of it, can I?"

"Nope." Her smile widened. "And thank you for not letting me win."

"You're welcome, I think."

"I'd better get back to work." She spun about and made

her way back to the house.

To his surprise, he watched her until the screen door slammed closed behind her. She really was one helluva woman.

CHAPTER FIVE

What was that expression her father used to say when Alice was a little girl: He was busier than a one armed paper hanger. That's pretty much the way she'd felt this last week. Extra runs into town, working side by side with the hands or her kids bringing the ranch back to life one step at a time. The routine was both exhausting and invigorating. Today, she felt especially old and tired. Were grandmothers supposed to work this hard?

Carson came bouncing down the stairs, hurried into the kitchen, grabbed a glass of juice from the table and guzzled it in one very long swallow. "No time to eat. There's a problem at the new development and I need to get there ASAP."

Instantly, she spun around and began slapping a breakfast sandwich together. "Hold your horses."

"Mom, I don't have time."

"Two seconds isn't going to kill you, but if you don't get some protein in you, that sugar rush you just inhaled will have you crashing in no time."

Carson knew better than to argue with his mother. All the kids knew when there was leeway and when Alice meant business, and right now, she meant business.

Wrapping the sandwich halfway in a paper towel, she handed it to her son. "Now, that didn't take long." She pushed up to her tippy toes and kissed him on the cheek. "Go fix whatever's wrong."

Taking a bite from the warm egg sandwich, he bobbed his head and muttered *Love you.*

"Don't talk with your mouth full," she hollered at his back. She loved having her grown children nearby. She'd gladly spend every minute of her day at the stove if it meant having a full table for meals. And most of the time, it was darn near bursting at the seams.

"Oh." Carson doubled back. "Clint didn't answer his cell. Let him know that I can't check fence lines and I got a call from the doc, some of our cattle are on their side of that fence."

She bobbed her head, wondering why their neighbor didn't call her. "Will do."

Once the door was shut and the kitchen cleaned up, she headed toward the barn. No surprise, she found Clint replacing worn leather on a bridle with the careful precision she'd come to expect from him.

The man lifted his head as she crossed through the open doors. "Mornin'"

"If you're looking for Carson, he had to go put out some fires."

Clint's eyes narrowed, his brows buckling into a perfect V.

"Figurative ones."

His expression easing, the man nodded and returned his attention to the work in front of him.

"So, looks like I'm your man for the day."

She couldn't swear to it, but she thought she noticed a tinge of a smile before his expression went blank and he raised his gaze to meet hers. "Horses are ready but if we've got fencing to fix, better take the four-wheeler."

"It'll make it easier to find the breach." A small sack in each hand, she lifted them like the scales of justice. "And I brought lunch."

Now his smile was wide and obvious. "Yes, ma'am."

An hour later, they were riding the fence line, stopping to get out and check posts and testing wire tension. Finally, up ahead, she spotted the problem. A section of downed fence. Hopping out of the vehicle, the two of them walked over to assess the situation. Shaking a loose post, she didn't like the way Clint had stopped walking, his gaze suddenly shifting from the downed section to some spot in the distance.

"What is it?" She moved to stand beside him.

"Tracks." His voice was tight, body suddenly alert in a way that put her on edge. He pointed to the ground. "No cow knocked this down. Someone's ridden through here."

Clear as day, right in front of them. Tire tracks, cutting across their land. Alice's hands fisted at her side. "Damn it. Not again."

"We'll have to round up the misplaced cattle, secure the fence, and then…" his voice slowed as he stared after where the tracks might lead.

Alice shook her head. "No. The cattle aren't going anywhere today. I want to see where these tracks are going."

Tension coursing through Clint was almost palpable. For a minute she thought he was going to argue, maybe take her back to the house, call the sheriff, but finally he nodded. "We'll ride alongside, far enough away not to disturb any evidence."

"Good idea." Climbing back into the four-wheeler, she was torn between wanting to catch the SOBs in action, and praying they were long gone by now.

The tracks seemed to go on forever. Eventually, they could see one of the old-line shacks ahead. Her mind ran through all the possible scenarios. Kids wanting a party place. Traveler looking for a cheap place to catch a good night's sleep. Or trouble. Heaven knew they'd had plenty of that.

When Clint came to a stop, she saw what he saw. The door slightly ajar. Oh, how she hoped it was teenagers. She was so tired of trouble.

"You'd better wait here a minute." Clint pulled a rifle from the back of the vehicle and handed it to her, then he grabbed another. "And whatever you do, don't shoot me."

Any other circumstance and she would have either laughed with him or reminded him that she could shoot an apple from a tree at twenty yards. As it was, she simply nodded, took hold of the gun, and kept her finger away from the trigger. She had no intention of shooting Clint, but if anyone else came out of that shed, she wasn't making any promises.

With no other vehicle in sight, Clint was pretty sure whoever had come around was probably long gone, but all it would take for assumptions to kill him was for one man to be left behind—armed. Quietly approaching the shack, he nudged the door open with his toe, thankful the hinges didn't squeak. His finger on the trigger, he eased inside, scanning the small area through the sight of the rifle. No one to his left. Kicking the door fully open, he whirled about bringing the other side into view. No one. He still wasn't finished. His back to the wall, he eased over to the closet that housed the toilet and sink. Taking in a deep breath, he slowly turned the knob and shoved the door open.

Lowering his weapon, he blew out a relieved sigh, disappointed he couldn't catch the intruder red-handed, and equally relieved he didn't have to kill anyone today. "Coast is clear, Ms. Sweet."

Alice crossed the threshold, her gasp startling him out of his thoughts. "Oh, Lord."

So intent on securing the shack from a human intruder, he'd barely taken note of the condition the shack was in. Several words came to mind, but the Lord's name wasn't one of them.

"Somebody was definitely looking for something." Alice righted a knocked over chair, and then another.

Unable to avoid stepping on shards of broken glassware and dishes, he righted the turned over table. "What I can't decide, is if they found it or not."

Feathers flew as they moved around the small space. Shaking her head, Alice hefted the slashed mattress back onto the metal framed cot. "They certainly left no corner unturned." She swiveled toward the wall of the narrow stove and sink that made for a kitchen, the oven door wide open. "Did they really think someone would hide something in an oven?"

"I don't know, but at least we know they weren't looking for another hay baler." Clint kicked a pile of trash to the side with his boot. These shacks were meant for emergencies like blizzards or injuries, only holding a military-style metal bunk bed, a table, two chairs, and non-perishable food items, including the required heaven's brew—coffee. Brooms and dust pans weren't standard materials.

Shaking her head, Alice surveyed the mess, her gaze suddenly narrowing, one finger lifting to point in his direction. "Which shack was that hay baler found in?"

Dang, that woman was smart. He should have thought of that. "This one."

"The cameras?" Her face lit up as if she'd found the leprechauns pot of gold.

Like he said, smart. Except for one thing. Looking up instead of around, there was no sign of any cameras. Hurrying outside, he quickly circled the small building. Nothing. Returning to where Alice stood staring at the doorway, he shook his head. "Gone."

"What do you mean, gone?"

He shrugged. "They must have spotted them. Taken them down. Not wanting us to view the SD cards inside."

"Don't they alert you when someone approaches? You know, like those fancy doorbells?"

How he hated to keep shaking his head at her. "Feature would be turned off or every armadillo and cow that meanders by would be sounding it off."

She heaved another sigh as she crossed the space, pulled her work gloves from her back pocket and retrieved a trash bag from a drawer by the sink.

"You don't have to do that. Benny and I will come back."

Raising one eyebrow, she glared at him as if he'd just kicked her puppy.

"Or we can do it now." He crossed to where she'd grabbed a garbage bag.

"Wait." She held her hand up. "What are the odds that something tossed around here has fingerprints? Maybe we should wait till the sheriff comes by to clean up."

He should have thought of that. Stopping mid-step, his

foot came down heavier than usual, a hollow sound catching his ear. He stomped on the floor, then took a single step to the side and stomped again. Both sounds hollow. Tilting his head, he listened carefully and moving to the next board, once again slammed the heel of his boot to the floor.

"Really, Clint. This is not the time for a jig."

"No, listen." He shook his head and stomped on the board he'd just hit, then moved several feet and stomped again. "Hear that?"

He had her attention. Squinting, she listened as he repeated the motions. "First one sounds hollow. The second one not so much. Like when Charlie would hammer at the wall listening for the hard sound of a stud instead of the hollow of sheetrock."

"Exactly." Would this woman ever cease to amaze him? Pulling his knife from his pocket, he unfolded the blade, and worked it into the narrow space. With a twist of his wrist, he applied pressure. The board lifted slightly. He slipped his fingers under the edge and pulled it up, revealing a dark space beneath.

Alice moved closer, bending to see.

The second board pulled up more easily, and then a third. Turning on the flashlight feature of his phone, he shone it inside. All he could see was a single canvas bag.

"What in the world?" Alice leaned even closer.

Reaching into the cavity, he gripped the dirty bag, yanking it from its hiding place, surprised by the weight of it. Setting it down on the floor between them, he opened the bag.

"My God." Alice's eyes grew wide and her hand flew to her mouth.

He pulled out one bundle of tightly wrapped bills, secured with rubber bands. Not bundles of single dollars, but hundred dollar bills.

Alice reached for another bundle and fanned the bills. Setting it aside, she did the same with another and then another. "There has to be tens of thousands of dollars."

"Or more," he added. "We'd better not touch anything else. You call the sheriff. Tell him we need him here."

She nodded. "I'm not moving until this shack is secure. I'm not losing this the way we lost the baler."

He sat quietly as she reported the find to the sheriff who promised to get there as fast as he could. Next she called Preston, then Garret. Each promised to phone the others and to meet her at the shack as soon as they could get to the ranch. That was one of the things he truly loved about this family. They had each other's backs, no matter what, no matter when. He had to wonder if Alice Sweet had any idea, despite the troubles brought on by his thieving predecessor, just how lucky she was.

CHAPTER SIX

Nervous energy had Alice cleaning every corner of her already clean kitchen. More specifically, the contents of her well-ordered cabinets were now scattered across the countertops while she wiped and scrubbed every shelf. She had to do something. The sheriff had been out in the line shack with the county crime scene techs. At first she'd stood around outside with Clint, watching, waiting. It hadn't taken long to realize despite the small space, a thorough processing was not going to be fast.

"Any word?" Rachel dropped her purse on the sofa and marched into the kitchen. "Oh my." Her gaze scanned the new mess Alice had made. "Bad news?"

"No news." Giving the top shelf one more wipe down, she slid back and heaved a frustrated sigh.

Rachel moved next to her mother. "Where's Clint?"

"He and Preston are at the line shack waiting for what Sheriff Boyd has to say. I got restless. Decided to clean out the cupboards."

"So I see." Rachel looked at the stacks of dishes to one side. "Shall I start putting some of this stuff back, or do you need help cleaning more shelves?"

For as long as she could remember, when life became too stressful, or too challenging, Alice would clean. For whatever reason, it helped her think. Though in this case there was nothing to think about, just a lot of waiting. "Yeah, I'm done."

Starting with the dinner plates, Rachel began stacking the dishes in the first cabinet, when the door swung open.

Preston wiped his boots and came in first, followed by the sheriff.

The lawman tipped his hat at her. "There are a few latent prints they were able to lift, but we doubt they're going to tell us much. Especially since any former employees could have left those prints at any point in time. The line shacks are for everyone."

She nodded. She'd thought of that herself.

"The good news is there's at least a hundred k in the sack."

For the first time all day, the urge to smile tugged at her cheeks. "That is good news." Very good news.

"Unfortunately, even though it's on your property, it could be evidence of a crime."

"So we don't get our money back?" Rachel asked.

The sheriff shook his head. "Eventually, yes, but for now, I have to impound it."

Two steps forward and one back. They'd made it this far with limited funds; a little while longer wasn't going to kill her. "What else are you thinking?"

The two men glanced back and forth at each other. Preston was the first to speak. "Ray or his men, someone, or some people, are lurking around."

"They know about the cameras too." Preston twirled the hat in his hand.

"You might want to try installing cameras that aren't obviously cameras," the sheriff suggested.

"Oh, yes." A plate in her hand, Rachel spun around to face everyone. "Like a nanny cam. No one realizes the teddy bear has a camera."

"Don't you think a Teddy bear would be a little out of place in a line shack?" Alice faced her daughter.

"She's on the right track." Preston raked his fingers through his hair and placed his hat on a nearby hook. "We should have thought to be more discreet."

Several handshakes, and back slaps, and promises were made to let them know as soon as the police knew anything as the sheriff left the house.

"I guess; now we wait." Preston sighed.

"And Clint?" Alice asked.

"He's overseeing the last of the crime scene people.

Then he said he was going to gather the cattle so he could fix the fence. I'd go help, but I have to get back to the office."

Alice nodded. "Good. We need to get the roaming cows off Doc's property." Stripping off her rubber gloves, she tossed them on the counter and decided with the cupboards cleaned out and Rachel putting everything away, working outside would be just the energy release she needed. "I'm going to go see about the fence."

Rachel's gaze dropped to her mother's. "Dressed like that?"

Glancing down at herself, Alice frowned. "Like what?"

"Mom, you're wearing your favorite housecleaning jeans."

"Okay…" Even though her daughter was right and she'd owned these pants since before she was married, it wasn't like they had holes in the knees or rips at the pocket. "The fence won't care."

Shaking her head, Rachel shrugged. "Well, if you don't care that you look like you fell out of a Monkey Ward's catalogue from a million years ago, I guess the fence won't either."

"Atta girl." She smiled at her daughter. The kid had a point, in the wide-legged pants reminiscent of bell-bottoms from her mother's era, she did indeed look a bit out of place. But then again, what did the fence care was spot on. "You finish up here and I'm going to get started."

"You shouldn't be working out there alone," Preston mentioned casually. Too casually. They all knew he was thinking of when she got tossed onto the fence by the spooked horse and had to wait for Brady to bring help.

"I'll have Brady with me, and Clint won't need long to round up a handful of cattle."

Preston and Rachel flashed a look at each other. Preston sighed and Rachel barely shrugged.

"I'll see you all for dinner." And with those few words, she was out the door, on her way to the old truck. With a quick nod, she'd tossed the large auger into the bed, then added several bags of cement, as well as new posts. Brady hopped into the front seat and they were off.

It didn't take long to reach the portion of downed fencing. Pulling up by the first fallen post, she pulled out the auger. It had been years, maybe decades since she'd handled one of these suckers, but she still remembered how it was done. Her plan was simple: dig all the holes now, and by the time Clint was finished rounding up the cattle, he could help set the posts. Working outside, in the fresh air, straining muscles she'd pretty much forgotten she had, all of it was an outstanding distraction.

Standing at the first spot, she positioned herself close enough to be able to both control and push on the auger. Easily, she set the choke, turned on the ignition, and pulled the start cord. First try, the thing almost danced away from her. It really had been a while since she'd done this. And the men always made it look so easy. There was no way she was going to let this hunk of curled metal get the best of her. Inching closer, she gripped the handles tightly and tried again. Only this time, she'd made one more miscalculation; always tuck wide-leg pants into her boots. Within seconds, the heavy equipment had started spitting dirt every which way before biting at her pant leg and threatening to knock her off balance.

She heard herself screech, felt the pressure of worn denim pulling at her. In a split second, the way a magician would whip a tablecloth out from under a fully set table, her favorite pants ripped away from her legs. She screeched again, Brady barked, and the hungry auger did as it was designed to do when hitting a rock, or apparently, pants; it shut off. Except now she found herself standing in her panties and boots in the middle of a field. And holy cow patties, was that the sound of a four-wheeler approaching? "Oh, crud."

Clint eased the four-wheeler along the fence, keeping the throttle where cattle would listen instead of scatter. He let the machine hum low and steady, arcing wide to turn the stubborn beasts that had scattered far and wide onto Doc's property. Finally, they were moving in the right direction, flowing back toward the gap like water trickling downhill.

Wind carried a sound that wasn't cattle. Metal coughing, then dying. He lifted off the throttle and let the herd walk, eyes running the line ahead. A figure appeared to be huddled by the fence—Alice, it had to be—but something was off. Hunched over, her arms moved in sharp, jerking motions. A sense of urgency gripped him. He couldn't explain why, but somehow he knew, something was very not right. Easing off the throttle, he let the cattle continue their plodding journey toward the fence opening, keeping his eyes on his boss and wishing cows moved more quickly.

As he drew closer he blinked, then blinked again. No longer crouched low to the ground, she now stood upright and if he wasn't mistaken, had a fantastic pair of legs. What he couldn't fathom is why the heck was she standing there with... he squinted, not shorts. What in the world? It wasn't until he was nearly upon her that he understood what he was seeing. Alice Sweet, ranch owner and mother of six, stood clutching what appeared to be her pants around her waist as if it were a towel and she'd just stepped out of the shower.

Glaring at the ground like a woman scorned, she lifted her chin and leveled her gaze with his as if daring him to say a word.

He killed the engine immediately, and climbed off. Keeping his gaze firmly on her face—and only her face—he approached cautiously. Brady circled them both, clearly agitated. "What happened?"

She huffed, adjusting her grip on the tattered fabric. "The auger happened. Started up fine, but these old pants..." She gestured with one hand before quickly grabbing the fabric again when it started to slip. "Let's just say the auger found them tastier than the dirt."

He followed her glance to the machine. The bit sat in fresh dirt, a collar of earth thrown up around it, and a blue ribbon of vintage denim tied into the flights. The engine was quiet. Thank God for clutches and kill switches that still remembered their job. His mind ran too freely to what could have been—bone, tendon, anything caught where cloth had gone. "You hurt?"

"Only my pride." She heaved a deep sigh. "Pro tip: wide-leg pants and augers are not on friendly terms."

He wasn't sure if he was more horrified at what could have gone wrong, or more amused at the ludicrous situation. Fighting the pull on his cheeks, he'd say amusement was winning out.

"I managed to get the pants unwound from the bit," she continued. "This was the best I could do to avoid scaring the cows with my bare legs."

Okay, so the woman's sense of humor held strong in all sorts of situations, even when her pride and propriety were at stake. Now he really had to fight the urge to smile. Removing the windbreaker he wore, careful to not let his eyes drop for another look at shapely legs, he handed it to her. "This might work better if you tie it around your waist. It should cover you better than those pants. And you won't have to hang on to it either."

Her free hand reached for the jacket. "Thank you."

Remembering his manners, he quickly spun on his heel, turning his back to her.

"Okay. Better. You can turn around now."

He did as he was told, allowing himself a quick peek. He'd never seen her in anything but slacks or a long dress at the parties for the kids' weddings. Neither had ever given him any hint that the woman had a great pair of gams.

"You're sure you're all right?" He kept his eyes on the tool.

"Bruised vanity. And chilly knees."

There was that sense of humor again. He bit back a smile.

She tilted her head at the strip of cloth still tied around the lower flights. "Dumb thing started, danced, then decided to eat my wardrobe."

He tried not to, he really did, but laughter bubbled over.

Alice rolled her eyes heavenward, which didn't help

him stop. He got it under control—almost—then lost it again when she deadpanned, "Put 'wide-leg pants' under the column labeled 'ranch hazards' on your next safety briefing."

"Yes, ma'am," he managed, breath finally cooperating. He wiped a palm over his face and got serious where he needed to. "I'll finish the holes. You sit in the truck, lock the doors, and pretend you're supervising."

"Pretend?" Only the smile flirting with the corners of her mouth belied her icy stare. Shaking her head, she turned on her heel and called over her shoulder, "You get started on the rest of the holes, I'll get my cell in the truck and have someone bring me a new pair of pants, then we'll both finish that fence."

How awful was it that the only thing he could think of at the moment was that woman sure knew how to wear his jacket?

CHAPTER SEVEN

Thank heaven for whoever invented the freezer. Then God bless the King family for coming up with the King Ranch casserole. After Alice's day today, the last thing she wanted to do was cook for a hungry brood. Heck, after the craziness of today, she wished she didn't have to sit down and eat with her family and could just climb under the covers and hide from her embarrassing escapade.

A seasoned rancher making such a stupid mistake as letting her wide leg pant get caught in the auger. Preston had already teased the dickens out of her when he delivered a fresh pair of straight-legged jeans from the laundry room. As sure as she was that her name was Alice Sweet, she knew that the teasing at dinner tonight would be relentless. And, most likely, well deserved.

"Hi Mom." Jillian came in the back door with her husband in tow and gave her a kiss on the cheek, then sniffed at the air. "Is that King Ranch casserole I smell?"

Alice nodded while ripping lettuce for a salad.

"Must have been a hard day." Jillian stood with Blake's arm around her waist.

For a second, Alice thought her daughter was being cute, but then she realized there was no teasing in the voice.

"You didn't hear?" Rachel looked around the crowded kitchen. "How did you not hear?"

"Hear what?" Standing by the double oven, Sarah Sue stopped transferring fresh rolls onto a plate, playfully smacking Preston's hand when he reached for one.

The smile they shared was almost enough to make Alice forget her miserable day. Returning her attention to the salad bowl, she let out a slow breath. Apparently, the Sweet Ranch grapevine was not living up to its usual speed of communication.

"Mom lost her pants in the field," Preston spoke, stone-faced.

"What?" Jillian spun around to stare at her mother. "How the heck does one lose their pants?"

"Not hard if you've had enough tequila," Rachel quipped.

Her mother and her sister's heads whipped around to glare at her.

Rachel raised her hand, palm open. "Hey, haven't you ever heard the song? 'Tequila Makes her Clothes Fall Off'?"

"I was not drunk." Stone-faced herself, Alice picked up the bowl and took a step toward the dining room. "I had a disagreement with an auger."

"An auger?" Jillian's voice rose several octaves. Jess and Cassie's concern echoed hers.

Sarah Sue sprang from the table where she'd sat down, reaching her mother-in-law in seconds. "Are you hurt? Let me see." She studied Alice from head to toe and was about to squat to check Alice's legs when Alice took a step back.

"I'm fine. It's my pants that didn't survive."

"Bet the cows enjoyed the show," Carson teased.

Preston looked to his brother. "I had no idea how good Mom would look wrapped in a windbreaker."

Biting down on her back teeth, Alice knew she had this coming, but that didn't mean she had to like it. Somewhere in the handbook of life it had to say one must never make fun of one's mother. It had to.

"When I got to the field with clean—straight leg—jeans, she was hiding in the car while Clint dug posts."

"Clint saw you without pants?" Jillian's eyes were wide as saucers.

"No, Clint did not see me without pants." Alice's response sounded too much like a whiny child for her own ears. "I had already wrapped myself in what was left of my jeans by the time he found me. Then he gave me his jacket for an easier cover up."

Now that she thought about it, Clint had been much more of a gentleman about all this than her own sons. At least when he sat down laughing, she knew he wasn't laughing at her so much as at the situation. And she suspected, there was a hint of nervous relief. Even she knew she could have been horribly injured, losing a limb or two and not just a pair of jeans. That guy had proven himself over and over with this family. From the day he showed up in her kitchen to inform her that something was terribly wrong and the hands had all left, to the day she got tossed onto the barbed wire, to today and everything in between.

"On the bright side," Preston reached into the silverware drawer, "we've got the budget for another hand. Benny's doing fine, and we did so well with the hay rotation thanks to Cassie, that we actually had enough extra to sell and help the bank accounts."

"I was pretty sure that would be the case." Carson smiled, carrying the stack of dishes to the dining room.

"Does this mean those of us with day jobs don't have to get up at the crack of dawn anymore?" Rachel pulled out the casserole. "Could someone close the oven door?"

"That's exactly what it means." Garret nodded. "Once the male calves are sold, we should be able to hire enough hands that we can all go back to focusing on our day jobs."

Alice moved to the dining room, pleased that she was no longer the brunt of the conversation, and very thankful for how hard everyone worked. Maybe she'd take a nice pie over to Clint. He really did handle today well. Actually, he handled pretty much everything well. Maybe two pies were in order.

Today had certainly been one hell of an interesting day. If anyone had told Clint that he would be out in the field today, surrounded by stray cattle and staring at Alice Sweet's legs with a little—okay, a lot—more interest than appropriate for a ranch hand—okay, foreman—to be ogling his employer, he would have told that person to stop smoking the funny stuff.

And yet, as he'd sat here trying to get lost in a dinner of reheated leftovers and a some benign program on TV, his mind kept wandering back to his boss's legs, to her general feistiness and overall entertaining sense of humor, and then to Carol. When they'd first met at the rodeo, she'd been the prettiest thing he'd seen in a very long time. Long black hair in a ponytail that hung down her back and swished about every time she laughed. Big blue eyes sparkled with delight and a hint of mischief. They probably should have dated longer than the whirlwind two months but he couldn't keep his hands off of her and spending the rest of his life with her at his side had felt like a pretty darn good idea. Less than a year later they'd had Jason.

At first it had been fun. The baby slept in a drawer of their dresser. They hadn't thought of it as poor but cute. Then things got crowded. And messy. And there was colic and teething and Carol had been at her wits' end. Clint, of course, had given up the rodeo scene as soon as she'd told him she was pregnant. It hadn't been a passion of his anyhow, just a means for extra money. He'd taken a job in town with a local construction company and had made decent money framing houses. With no choice, they'd moved into a bigger apartment and then as Jason grew and Carol became more and more critical and, well, nagging, he took on a second job and they moved into a house. Things had gotten so bad that he could see it in Jason's face when he came home and the screaming and fighting would start. He hated it. Hated that he couldn't make peace with his wife, couldn't make everyone happy. Every so often she'd be smiling and laughing like the woman he'd fallen in love with and then suddenly, facing a deranged fire-breathing dragon would have been easier. He'd begun to wonder if perhaps she was bipolar or something, but there was no getting her to see anyone.

Shaking his head, his mind jumped back to Alice. With all the horrible things that happened to her in the last few years, he couldn't imagine her ever losing it the way Carol would. Heaving a sigh, he reached for the manila envelope he'd taken out of the nightstand by his bed. It had sat on the table taunting him through dinner and some rerun of a reality TV show that reminded him why the television had once been called the idiot box. Not for the first time over the years, he'd dumped all the clippings onto the table and began reading. A knock at the door pulled him away. "Come in."

The wooden door squeaked open and Alice Sweet appeared in the doorway. "Am I interrupting?"

He shook his head, pushed to his feet, and quickly gathered the clippings into a single pile. "Of course not. Come on in."

A smile on her face, the woman should have looked exhausted after the day she'd had, but she looked…radiant. "I got tired of being on the receiving end of my children's sense of humor and decided you deserved a reward for not poking fun at my stupidity."

"Miss Alice, you are many things, but stupid isn't one of them."

"Tell that to the auger and my favorite old jeans." Not till she extended her hands did he notice she carried a foil-covered pie. "Thought you might like dessert."

"That's very thoughtful of you."

She shook her head. "Selfish. I've got a sweet tooth and didn't want to behave like a sulking kid eating pie in my room."

He lifted the foil off the pie and realized it was still warm. "I can't picture you ever sulking."

"I have my days." Her smile remained intact as she glanced around the place, down at the table and then back up.

"Where are my manners? Would you care to join me for a slice?"

Her smile brightened. "Thank you, that would be nice. Sweet tooth, you know."

He chuckled. "So I've heard."

Placing the pie dish on the nearby counter, he pulled out

two plates, then carefully cutting two slices, he turned, a plate in each hand, and almost dropped them when he saw her reading the top clipping. His throat tightened and his palms began to sweat. If she put two and two together, he could lose the best job he'd ever had. The closest thing to family he'd had in a very, very long time. Too long.

"I used to tease my Rachel she had a thing for tragic deaths. That kid would watch the *Selena* movie, the *La Bamba* movie, and *Titanic* so often, I wondered what the heck had I done wrong."

He set one dish in front of her.

"You have dreams of being a detective or something?"

"Detective?"

She tugged the top clipping off the pile. "Yeah. Here." She pointed to the story of a man convicted for the death of his wife, then moved her finger over to the next column and byline. "And here. One woman is found dead in a fire, and then a man is found dead from carbon monoxide poisoning. Do you suspect like the arson victim, it wasn't an accident?"

Now he was completely confused. Reaching for the clipping, he looked at the story she'd pointed to.

"You're frowning."

"I, uh, was just thinking." He straddled his seat like a man on a horse, poking at the pie with his fork. Scared to look up. "How much do you know about me?"

The sound of her fork touching the plate had him sneaking a peek at her. To his surprise, she was smiling at him. "You mean, did I look at your employment application?"

He nodded.

"I did. Right after I found out Ray had been swindling me."

"Then you know?" He swallowed hard, almost choking on the barely chewed morsel of pie.

"That you're an ex-con?" One brow rose up a little higher than the other before her head bobbed.

"Do you know what I was convicted of?"

She shook her head. "I'll be honest. It was a while after

Ray took off with so much of our money before I got around to looking at your paperwork. I'd given the sheriff what I had on the others who took off, but didn't look at yours right away because you were still here. By the time I did go through more of the paperwork trying to get a handle on what the heck was going on, I had already gotten to know you. Knew I could trust you, so I didn't really care what you'd done."

"What if I'd killed someone?"

Her lips pressed into a thin line, she tilted her head, staring at him with eyes that felt as if they could read deep down to his soul. "Did you?"

CHAPTER EIGHT

nyone else and Alice would have been sitting on pins and needles waiting for the response. No, she would have been poised to spring to her feet and bolt for the door, perhaps wishing she'd brought keys or a gun for self-defense. But that wasn't the case. She knew deep down, as surely as she knew her name was Alice Sweet, that the answer would be no.

Clint shook his head. "I did not. But the police and the jury seemed to think I did."

"Want to tell me about it?"

His fingers glazed over the clipping in front of him with a gentleness that seemed more appropriate for petting the family cat than for a piece of paper. After a long silence, she thought he was going to say no. Instead he kept his gaze on the paper and proceeded to tell her how he'd met his wife, and the troubles they'd had. "I read over these clippings, hoping I will notice something, anything, that will prove I did not set my house on fire to kill my wife."

As he spoke, her gaze dropped to the clippings; *House fire claims life of local woman. Husband arrested for murder of wife. Man convicted of arson and manslaughter in the death of his wife.* When he brought up his son Jason, her attention darted over to the framed photo. "Would that be you and Jason?"

For the first time since he started talking, he pulled his gaze away from the page and looked to where she pointed. His head bobbed. "He was only six in that photo. He was ten when… when Carol died. He went to live with Carol's Aunt Agnes."

She listened as he seemed to relive that night,

explaining about going out for a drink to get away from the fighting. To coming home and falling asleep on the sofa. Waking up to the smell of smoke and the flickering flames. How he managed to save Jason but despite every effort, couldn't get back upstairs to Carol. Every few moments Alice nodded her head, her heart breaking for this good man who was clearly in so much pain merely recounting the history. She couldn't fathom what he'd gone through at the time, and fought to keep her hands on the table and not reach out to pat his arm or hold his hand. Instead, she merely sat and listened.

"Finding work back in Wyoming would have been hard enough as an ex-con, but there wasn't a soul on the planet who hadn't heard about the case and no one wanted to hire a wife killer." His gaze remained on the paper in front of him as he momentarily closed his eyes before going on. "I had to come all the way to Texas to find work and even then, it was never anything long term, or well paying. I slept a lot in my truck. Until Ray. He didn't seem to care. Said everyone deserved second chances. I believed him. Was thankful. More than thankful."

Once upon a time, she would have expected Ray to do the noble thing. The Ray they all thought they knew.

He gave a short-deprecating snort. "My guess is he hired me because he thought I'd be as crooked as the rest of the hands and willing to go along with his plans."

"You. Knew?" She could barely get the words out.

His head shook from side to side. His head back, he closed his eyes again. "No. But I must have done enough right for him to know that I was honest. It probably didn't hurt that once when we were talking over a fence post, he asked me questions about what I'd done. I doubt telling him I was innocent was what he'd wanted to hear."

If she could have, she would have kicked herself for even considering that he might have known what Ray was doing and not said a word. That went against everything she'd learned about him. She only hoped he didn't hold her momentary lapse against her.

"Jason's grown up thinking his father murdered his

mother. I've tried to reach out to him, but, he's refused any contact with me. I can't give up, though. I have to prove to my son that no matter how it looks, what anyone says, I would never have done that to Carol, no matter how bad it got."

Listening to the many times he'd tried to speak to his son, tried to find a way to prove his innocence, she wanted to jump up and pull him into a tight embrace the way she would any wounded child and reassure him everything would be okay, but he wasn't a child, and she doubted that even vindication could make all these lost years right again.

"And now, you know as much as I do." For the first time since he'd looked at the photo, lifting his head, he turned his eyes to hers. "Am I fired?"

She actually rolled her eyes at him. "Not only won't I fire you, but if you actually kill someone, I'd be willing to bet that not only did they deserve it, I'd help you bury the body." Letting a smile tease at her lips, she added, "We have an awful lot of land out here."

Though he didn't fully crack a smile, his cheek twitched and the darkness in his eyes seemed to give way to a teeny sparkle. "Thank you."

"So." Blowing out a deep breath, she straightened in her seat. "What are we going to do about this?"

"We?"

She nodded. "You're my best hand, a much respected foreman, and, I hope, friend. How can I help?"

If Clint had thought Alice Sweet just short of an angel, he was pretty sure at this moment she was indeed a saint. "I don't know that you can." His gaze dropped to the clipping he'd been fingering like a lifeline to his sanity. Always so focused on the mentions of his case, he'd never even noticed the other articles. Not only was the man dead, but the man was his next-door neighbor. What didn't make sense to him was that the guy next door had just replaced his gas furnace the year before. How odd was that?

"What is it?"

He glanced up at her. "What is what?"

"You have a look in your eye that I see when something is bothering you. Not that being falsely convicted isn't reason enough to be bothered, but there's something else."

Did this woman really know him so well? Staring at her for a moment, it struck him that at this point, she knew so much, how could it hurt to tell her what he was thinking? After all, how much worse could he look to her? "I never noticed that my neighbor died shortly after my house burned down."

Her gaze darted to the clipping before she edged it out from under his finger and read it to herself. "The carbon monoxide death was your next-door neighbor?"

He nodded.

"And this happened right after your house burned down?"

"Except his was considered an accident and mine was determined to be arson."

Eyes narrowed, she read the article again, then eyes wide open, leveled her gaze with his. "I'm not a detective, and maybe I've watched too many crime shows on television that have no basis in reality, but this says he was found on the floor of his garage with the engine running."

Clint pulled the article back. He had assumed when he saw carbon monoxide that it was a furnace. Scanning as quickly as he could, he said, "The only reason it wasn't deemed a suicide was because the spring on the door was broken so the investigators determined that it was an accident. That he was most likely trying to manually open the door before he gave up and the fumes overtook him before he could turn off the engine and get some fresh air."

"What do you know about your neighbor?" she asked.

"Apparently, not enough." Could there be a connection? Had the clue to his innocence been in the manila folder all this time? Or was he grasping at straws again?

Alice pulled out her phone and began tapping at the screen. Her chin lifted and she glanced at the article before turning back and tapping some more.

"What are you doing?"

"Looking up the guy's name. Seeing what I can find." She scrolled through the screen, her finger moving, then pausing as she read, then swiping at it again.

"Find anything relevant?"

"Hard to say." She squinted and he wished he could read her mind. "Was he divorced?"

Clint shrugged. "I know we would occasionally hear him and his wife arguing if we were both in our kitchens at the same time. I remember thinking maybe married people aren't supposed to get along. That maybe my parents were the exception to the rule, and not the norm."

"That's right. You mentioned your parents balanced each other."

He nodded, and even smiled. "They were like two peas in a pod."

"That's nice." Alice smiled. "So he was married."

It wasn't a question, but he responded anyhow. "Except we hadn't seen his wife for a while."

"What's a while?"

"At least a few weeks, maybe a month or more. We figured she was visiting a relative or something."

"Hmm." She returned to scrolling. "Well, well."

"What?" He inched closer. Close enough to smell the vanilla in her hair. Crazy. He shouldn't be noticing her shampoo.

"When I type in the address, it comes up that it was bought in foreclosure."

He shrugged. "Makes sense if the guy died unexpectedly."

"No." She shook her head. "It was sold on the courthouse steps only a couple of weeks after he died. That had to be in the works long before he died. Trust me, if anyone knows about the threat of foreclosure, it's me."

"Do you think all of this could be connected?"

Her mouth clamped shut, she tapped some more at her phone and nodded. "And I know just the person to help us figure this out."

Could it be after all this time, something had finally gone right for him?

"Declan, hello. It's Alice Sweet." She put the call on speaker.

"Ms. Alice, what a nice surprise."

"I'm not calling too late, am I?"

"Nope. Only ranchers go to bed with the chickens."

She laughed. "True. Listen, you've got people working on finding Ray, right?"

"The police are doing all they can—"

"No." She cut him off. "I mean someone else outside of law enforcement."

"That would be Brooklyn. The best of the best and even he's having trouble tracking this character down, but I promise you, if anyone can find him, it's Brooklyn. As a matter of fact, I think one of your sons is talking to him about some security set up at the ranch. Since finding that money."

"Yes, of course. But I'd like his number, if you don't mind." Her gaze shifted from the phone screen to Clint. "I have something else I'd like him to look into."

Clint's hands fisted at his side. Not from anger, but from the restraint it took not to spring up in his seat and shout hallelujah. Not only did someone—Alice—believe in him, but maybe somewhere out there, someone who actually knew what they were doing, and not just sulking over old clippings, would dig into the truth. Because the truth was, someone set his house on fire, and that someone was not him.

CHAPTER NINE

Going over her list for her call to Declan's friend Brooklyn, Alice glanced up as Garret came through the back door. Though he was far from being a little boy, he had that same look a kid might have when he's about to confess he's the one who broke the neighbor's window when he was supposed to be doing chores. Lingering by the counter, his hesitant smile suggested he wanted something from her.

"Coffee?" she offered.

"Thanks, Mom." He accepted the mug she handed him, taking a long sip before setting it down. "Do you remember how I told you the kids at school took a vote and decided they wanted this year's dance to be a fifties styled event?"

She bobbed her head. "Didn't someone watch an old musical with June Allyson or Jane Powell or something?"

Swallowing another sip, he nodded. "And I think *Back to the Future* too because they chose the name Enchantment Under the Sea."

"How original." She chuckled. "The dance is tomorrow night, right?"

"Right." He heaved a deep sigh and Alice looked up, her list for Brooklyn nearly forgotten. "Just spit it out. What's wrong?"

He picked up the mug again. "Since the dance is in the gymnasium, the kids can't start decorating too early."

"Makes sense."

"And under normal circumstances, decorating would have been finished in plenty of time."

Any fool would recognize that the non-normal circumstances were about to be explained.

"With the exception of the new girl in town, Mary Borden, and Jimmy Kendall, the rest of the planning and decorating committee are home with the same bug."

"All of them?" That would be too much coincidence.

"All of them. Sunday after church, all the committee members got together to finalize the plans. Apparently, Mary and Jimmy are the only two with phenomenal constitutions because everyone else is sick as a dog."

"I'm very sorry to hear that." She really was. Putting all that work into planning the perfect dance and then to be stuck home sick and miss it all.

"Sorry enough to help?" He flashed a shaky smile. Oh, how at this moment he looked so like her mischievous little boy.

"Maybe. What do you need?"

"Everything."

Her brows lifted and brain stopped computing. "Say again."

"They haven't done anything. I only found out an hour ago when Kate Hall called to tell me that she was coming down with something too and the ball was in my court."

"So when was all this decorating supposed to have happened?"

"After school yesterday and today."

The back door creaked, and hat in his hand, Clint came in, cleaning his boots on the heel scraper. "Mornin'"

"Morning, Clint." Alice waved to the coffee pot. "Help yourself to a cup. We'll be done here in a minute or two."

Garret looked over at Clint, his brows buckled in thought. "You're pretty good with wood."

Coffee mug in hand, Clint turned to face him. "Sometimes. You need something fixed?"

"More like made."

Clint nodded. "What did you have in mind?"

"A dance."

Now the man looked from Garret to Alice and back, but didn't say a word.

Since Garret was equally as silent as Clint, Alice spoke up. "Seems that there's a school dance tomorrow and no decorations yet. The theme is Enchantment Under the Sea. I've been recruited to help and I'm guessing now you are too."

Garret nodded and Clint just stared.

"If it's asking too much…" Garret shook his head.

"Well," Clint set the mug he'd yet to sip on the counter, "I suppose, if you tell me what you want, I can sure try."

"That's my man."

Alice couldn't agree with her son more. Seems Clint was making a habit of coming to the Sweet's rescue.

Garret pushed to his feet. "I'm going to be late if I don't get going. The sooner you can get to the school the better. Mary and Jimmy are being excused from classes, but I have no idea how much they'll be able to get done. I'm going to try and round up some more kids with a little artistic talent, but frankly, you're my ace in the hole."

"I don't know about that. But, thankfully, with Benny to handle things here, we'll both be there as soon as we can."

"Thanks, Mom." Garret leaned over and kissed his mother on the cheek. "You're the best."

Even though she knew he was just buttering her up, she giggled nonetheless. "Flattery will get you everywhere."

Her son waved at Clint and went out the front door.

Alice retrieved her list. "I called Declan this morning and he gave me Brooklyn's number. I figure you should be here when I call in case he has any questions I can't answer."

"Makes sense," Clint nodded.

Her phone rang, giving her a start. Looking down, the name made her smile. "Hey, Son."

"Morning, Mom." She could hear the smile in Kade's voice. "Listen, I'm coming home next weekend and want to surprise Cassie."

"She'll like that."

"Yeah, but I'm bringing a buddy with me."

"Oh,"

"Since we've got a house full again, I thought I'd better make sure that was okay."

"You know it is. I'm always happy to have our

military's finest. And I won't say a word to Cassie."

"Thanks, Mom. They're calling me. I have to go. Love you."

"Love you back." Still smiling at the phone, she slipped it into her pocket. "All right. Let's call Brooklyn."

For a small town, the gym that serviced both the junior high and high school was pretty impressive. To the opposite side of the large hall, the two kids hovered by a stack of poster board like they'd been told to build Rome with a glue stick. Another kid wobbled on a ladder in a dangerous attempt to tape blue streamers in the corner of the gym. Any minute now Clint expected to see the kid topple sideways taking the ladder, the streamers, and his dignity down with him. And possibly breaking a bone along the way.

Alice came strolling in behind him, her gaze darting from one side of the ample space to the other. When her gaze landed on the kid standing tip toe on the highest rung of the ladder, her brows dipped in a frown, her hand fisted on her hips, and her voice bellowed under the cavernous space. "Martin Folsom, you get off that rickety ladder this minute."

One of the things he'd found delightful about Honeysuckle, besides the quirky title of Corn Hole Capital of the state, when it came to small-town friendliness, it pretty much took the prize. Everyone knew everyone, but more importantly, everyone seemed to look out for each other as well.

"But," the kid waved an end of the crepe streamer at the woman, "I'm almost done."

"Correction." Alice pointed a finger at him. "You are done."

With a heavy sigh, the kid made it back down the ladder, the other two over by the posters having watched the exchange with surprising interest.

"So." Alice smiled at all the kids now looking at her

with gripping attention. "What is the plan?"

The three heads turned to face each other and Clint got the distinct impression that not a single one had a clue what they were supposed to be doing. Though it shouldn't have been funny, he found himself biting the inside of his cheeks not to chuckle.

"Well," the only girl, probably Mary, spoke up, "we're supposed to be coloring waves on the poster to put on the walls, but Callie is the artist and she's home sick."

"I think I can help." Alice nodded her head.

Clint had to blink. So the woman could run a ranch, a family, train dogs, and draw? Maybe some day he would stop being surprised by this lady.

"Where are the paint supplies?" Alice scanned the floor area where the two kids had been working.

"We hadn't gotten that far. We were told we could use whatever supplies were in the art room."

"All right. Who's going to show me the way?"

Mary grinned enthusiastically. "Follow me."

Taking in the few supplies that were scattered around, Clint's gaze landed on a box overflowing with papers, and streamers, and what looked like cut out fish. Thinking through the theme, he lifted his eyes heavenward and studied the ceiling.

"In the movie they had seahorses, fish, and other fun glittery stuff hanging from the ceiling." The kid, Jimmy, was staring up as he spoke. "We thought we could put some up on the walls, that would be kind of close."

Clint nodded. Then pointed to the container of decorations. "Let's see what we have to work with."

The two rummaged through the container he'd seen and another off to the side. Most of the items were scattered on the floor now so they could take inventory when Alice and Mary came back.

Pushing a rolling cart overloaded with what he assumed were art supplies. Alice grinned at him. "Everything we could possibly want to transform this place."

The way Jimmy, Mary and Martin glanced at each other, Clint was pretty sure that they weren't convinced.

Alice must have noticed their reaction as well, because she turned to him and raised a single brow. She didn't say a word, and yet, he was pretty sure he knew what she wanted.

He nodded ever so slightly. Yeah, he was full in. "Is there any spare wood in this place? Like plywood?"

Jimmy shrugged. "Maybe in the shop. They teach kids woodworking."

"Then we're going to start with some decent waves. Show me where the shop classes are and we'll cut some real waves, create depth to hide that stage up there."

The kid looked to where he'd pointed then back.

"And Martin," she tipped her head toward the doorway, "go ask the custodian if he has a better ladder than that old wobbly thing."

Martin nodded and took off running.

"Walk," Alice shouted. "You're no good to me if you break a leg or wind up in detention." The kid instantly slowed but still scurried along.

"What do you want me to do?" Mary Borden stood eagerly awaiting instructions.

"We," Alice linked elbows with the new to town teen, "are going to start creating the enchantment."

By the time Clint returned to the gym with the cut-out sheets of wave-shaped plywood, Alice and Mary had already created a slew of sea creatures. Jimmy was up on a sturdy ladder hanging balloons painted like fish in every color imaginable.

A few hours later, Garret showed up with a few boxes of pizza and a six-pack of soda. Looking up as he walked, he let out a sharp whistle. "Wow."

Clint had to admit, they'd accomplished more than he'd expected, or could have hoped.

"Good." Alice stood from the makeshift table where she was sprinkling glitter on strips of seaweed they'd been taping to the wall, and stretched her back left then right. "You're just in time to help with the streamers."

Her son gave her a dip of his chin and a wide salute. Between bites of pizza and sips of cola the small group worked, laughed, and in the end, gave a sea of high fives.

"This looks pretty darn good for," Alice looked down at her watch, "for only nine hours work. The paint on the waves will be fully dry by morning."

"Thank you, Mrs. Sweet." Mary turned around and offered her hand to Clint. "You too, Mr. Sweet."

Jimmy and Martin's jaws dropped, and their eyes bugged, but Alice and Garret seemed to take the confusion in stride. Clint, on the other hand, was struck dumb. What the heck was he supposed to say?

"Mary," Garret waved to Clint, "this is our foreman, Clint Gibbons."

"Oh," the girl blushed, "sorry."

"No worries." Alice smiled at her. "Soon enough you'll know everyone in town." Alice leaned in conspiratorially, "And they'll all know you."

He wasn't sure if she looked more flabbergasted at her mistaking him for a Sweet or the idea that everyone in town would know her business.

"Hey," Martin looked up, "my mom is outside. She's giving us all rides home."

"Y'all run on. We'll see you tomorrow night." Garret waved at their backs. When they'd left the room, he turned to face his mother and Clint. "Since y'all are being so helpful, we're short chaperones for tomorrow night."

"I thought those days were behind me." Alice chuckled.

Garret shrugged. "Please?"

His mom nodded. "I guess it won't kill me."

"Good." He turned to face Clint. "And you?"

He turned to his boss. "If I can hitch a ride. Why not?"

CHAPTER TEN

Considering how many dresses Alice pulled out of her now small closet, anyone would think she was still in high school and this was her class dance instead of her being a full-grown adult with grandchildren.

A whistle sounded behind her. "Looking good." Her son Preston stood in the doorway smiling. "Don't think I've seen you this dressed up since, well, I don't remember when."

"Thank you." She took one last look in the mirror and decided she wouldn't embarrass anyone in her family, as long as she didn't trip over her own two feet. Hopefully walking on four inch heels would be like riding a bike—you never forget.

"For what it's worth, your date is waiting downstairs."

"My what?" She spun around.

"Clint."

Rolling her eyes, she shook her head at her son. "Really, Preston."

"Hey, you razzed us enough when we were in high school. I figure this is probably my last chance."

Sons. She doubted they'd ever outgrow that locker room humor. "Making you wear your tie straight and combing your hair does not count as razzing."

Smiling like a young boy with that glint in his eyes, he merely shrugged before pushing away from the door jamb. "Seriously, Mom. You look great."

"Thank you."

At the bottom of the stairs, Clint stood chatting with Cassie. Like every ranch hand on the planet, the man wore jeans and boots and cotton shirts, flannel in the winter.

Tonight, he had on boots, but these were unscuffed and polished, and a jacket and tie. What was commonly known as the Texas tuxedo. And boy did this man know how to wear it.

"Ready to face the den of teenagers?" His smile was slight, and his voice smooth as honey.

"As ready as I'm going to be."

"Where's Garret? Thought he was meeting us here to ride together."

She shook her head. "He and Jackie left early. Said they'd meet us there."

Clint nodded and to her surprise, extended his elbow to her. "Shall we?"

For some reason, it took longer than it should have to extend her hand and curl her fingers around his forearm. It was silly, really. The gesture meant nothing more than old-fashioned chivalry, like helping an old woman across the street. But still, it felt somehow very personal. Once they reached the truck, Clint opened the door for her, something he'd done more than once in the many months he'd worked on the ranch, and yet, just like the extended arm, this felt really different. Not awkward, not unpleasant, just, different—and nice.

The conversation in the truck went like any other chit-chat any other day. There was no mention of anything serious; not Ray, not Brooklyn, not the financial challenges, nothing.

"I had no idea you were so talented." Clint kept his eyes on the road.

"Doesn't take a lot of talent to paint a few fish and waves."

"Depends on how you look at it. I could have painted the waves. There would have been one shade of blue and that would have been it. Maybe I would have painted one cutout a darker shade and another a lighter shade, but I promise you there would not be shadows, and white froth or anything else to make the waves look like we were standing on a beach in Galveston or Padre."

She shrugged. "Art was a favorite class of mine in high

school. Mrs. Halinan, now that woman had talent. Not the paint waves and fish kind but the sell your paintings in an art show kind of talent. If not for her patience, and instructions, and interest, my waves would have been plain just like yours."

"I guess that explains the fish too."

This time she chuckled. "I think it's safe to say we can give Mrs. Halinan the credit for that too."

"Did you help your kids with their art projects?" He stole a quick glance in her direction before returning his attention to the road ahead.

"Not really. With six kids, they usually helped each other. Charlie and I would help with math and science, but art wasn't a big thing." They arrived at the school and Clint pulled around to the teacher's parking lot as Alice suggested. She really had enjoyed working on the gym yesterday. Maybe she should take up painting, not walls, but pictures, for a hobby. She shook her head at her own thoughts—who the heck had time for a hobby?

Clint met her on the passenger side of the truck. "What's wrong?"

"Wrong?"

"You're shaking your head."

"Oh." She chuckled. "Don't let that worry you. I spend a lot of my spare time talking myself out of all sorts of crazy ideas."

This time he didn't extend his arm, and to her surprise, she felt a bit... disappointed. Thankfully, the disappointment disappeared the minute she crossed the threshold into the old gym. She'd thought everything looked great when they'd left yesterday, but tonight, with the overhead lights off and only dim lights on the perimeter and colored lights directed and the floating fish and urchins hanging over head, the place looked magical. Maybe she would find some time to paint. Maybe.

✦

"Holy cow. Did it look this good when we left last night?" Clint cast a quick glance from one end of the gym to the other. The place looked spectacular. Better than the movie they were trying to mimic. Though he had to do a double take at the attendees. Many of the girls seemed to have fallen out of the original movie, wearing form-fitting dresses with wide skirts that twirled when they danced.

Alice Sweet shook her head. "I think it's just the magic of the night."

She had a point. This place held the kind of magic you only saw in movies, and certainly not something he'd expected from a handful of high schoolers. Still. "You, Mrs. Sweet, are too humble. But I have to agree, there is some sort of magic in the air tonight. I hope these kids appreciate the hard work that you and the other kids put in."

"And you," she added.

He bobbed his head. "And me."

"Martin did a good job with the spotlights," Alice murmured beside him, a soft smile on her face. Colored lights played across the waves he'd cut, shadows lifting and falling like the ocean was breathing. Alice's seahorses floated above, a little parade that made even the teachers smile when they looked up.

"He did," Clint agreed, though his gaze was less on the decorations and more on Alice. He'd seen her covered in mud, paint, and hay. He'd seen her work until her back ached and her hands were raw. But this—this polished, graceful woman—was a side of her he'd not seen before. Not even during the last-minute receptions for a couple of her kids.

Music thumped, then slid into something old he remembered from his grandmother's record collection. Garret appeared at their side. "I know this isn't Mom's first turn at chaperone, but just in case, what you need to look for is—"

Clint cut him off. "Unusual activity around the punch bowl, huddles in the corner, both of which can mean there's liquor around, and, of course, the Noah's Ark effect."

It took Garret a few minutes to connect the dots and

burst out in a single loud laugh. "Never heard it put quite that way."

"When I was in high school and my mom would let me have a party, her post was usually by the main floor bathroom. I can still see her standing arms crossed, shaking her head, smiling, and repeating, 'Only one at a time.'"

"Okay. Then I'm off to wander the grounds and the parking lot. Make sure Noah isn't busy out there either." Walking away, Garret continued to chuckle to himself.

"The bathroom, huh?" Alice smiled up at him.

He shrugged. "What can I tell you, kids weren't too bright in my day."

Her gaze shifted to the kids on the dance floor and she barely shook her head. "Somehow, I doubt that."

Twenty minutes in, the music shifted to the unofficial anthem of the fifties—"Rock Around the Clock." A few brave souls ventured onto the dance floor, awkwardly trying steps that hadn't been popular for decades. Clint found himself tapping his foot, memories of his mother teaching him to dance in their kitchen surfacing unexpectedly. That's when he spotted them—two boys lingering by the refreshment table, looking around with exaggerated casualness that screamed *up to no good*. One nudged the other, and a small silver flask appeared from inside a jacket.

Clint moved without hurry, positioning himself beside them before they could make their move. "Evening, gentlemen."

The boys froze, the flask hastily disappearing back into the jacket.

"Evening," the taller boy attempted nonchalance. "Great decorations."

"Thanks. Put those waves together myself." He nodded toward the boy's jacket. "That wouldn't happen to be something you're planning to add to the punch, would it?"

Their expressions would have been comical if he weren't genuinely concerned. The shorter boy looked ready to bolt, while the taller one's face cycled through denial, defiance, and finally, resignation.

"Look," Clint lowered his voice, "I'm not going to drag

you to the principal or call your parents." He extended his hand, palm up. "But I can't let you spike the punch."

After a moment's hesitation, the flask appeared and with clear reluctance, was paced firmly in Clint's open hand.

"You ever been drunk, boys?" Clint pocketed the flask.

They exchanged glances, then shook their heads.

"First time's never as fun as you think it'll be." He smiled slightly. "Especially not when you're surrounded by teachers and parents."

"You gonna tell our folks?" the shorter boy asked.

Clint considered this. "No. But I expect to see you both at the Sweet Ranch next Saturday morning. I've got some fence posts that need painting. Six hours ought to cover it."

Relief washed over their faces, followed by confusion. "That's it?" the taller one asked.

"That's it. Now go ask some girls to dance. That takes more courage than drinking ever will."

As they walked away, looking chastened but not humiliated, Clint wondered if Jason had ever tried something similar. A familiar pang of loss hit him, sharper than usual. He'd missed so much. He should have been there for his son. To chaperone the dances, coach the ball games, give advice on girls, cheer at graduations, toast his first job, first promotion. Shoulda, coulda, woulda.

"Everything all right?" Alice's voice broke through his thoughts.

"Fine." He straightened. "Just preventing a punch bowl disaster." He held up the confiscated flask. "This'll stay with me for now. The two culprits will be doing chores at the ranch this Saturday."

"Well handled." Her gaze followed the direction he discreetly pointed to two boys hovering along the edge of the dance floor. "I'll make sure their parents know they'll be expected at the ranch. Sometimes kids need consequences, but not always public humiliation."

The song changed, another number that Clint recognized from his grandparents' record collection— "Earth Angel." Several couples moved to the center of the floor, arms awkwardly wrapped around each other, swaying more than dancing.

"Would you like to dance?" The question was out before he could think better of it.

Alice's eyes widened slightly, but her smile never faltered. "I would."

Holding her hand in his should have been more awkward. His other hand around her waist, and the entire stance felt oddly at home. The first step, and he realized immediately that Alice Sweet, among other things, knew how to dance. They sashayed around the floor, twirling her out and in a few times, always returning her to the fold of his arms.

"You're very good. Better than Charlie. Bless that man, so many qualities, dancing wasn't his best."

"My grandmother will thank you. She insisted she'd taught my dad how to dance and she could teach me. And so she did."

"And quite well." The song came to an end and Alice stepped back. "We'd better get back to making sure these kids stay on the straight and narrow."

He bobbed his head. "You go left, I'll bank right."

Her chin dipped as her smile widened. "See you around."

The rest of the evening flew by with little trouble. Though if he were honest with himself, he'd kept hoping for another opportunity for at least one more dance. He hadn't danced in years, decades more like it, but tonight he'd had more fun over a single dance than he could remember. Apparently, there was a lot about Alice Sweet and her family that was contributing to the best life he'd ever had. On the ride home they shared stories of mean girls, nice girls, daring boys, and the reassuring idea that for the most part, chivalry is not dead in this part of Texas.

Spitting up gravel despite the slow ride down the front drive, he pulled the truck to a stop in front of the Sweet home. Circling the hood of the vehicle, he managed to get to Alice's door before she climbed out. Or maybe she'd waited for him. He wasn't totally sure. Tempering his smile, he took a step back. "Thanks for including me tonight."

"My pleasure. I had a nice time. Thank you."

"Any time." He recognized he not only meant it, but hoped she'd take him up on it. And how foolish was that?

CHAPTER ELEVEN

The timer on the oven dinged just as tires crunched up the drive. Alice slipped on an oven mitt and pulled out a pan of bar cookies, the caramel still bubbling at the edges. Brady, asleep under the table a heartbeat ago, shot to his feet with a single sharp woof and tore for the door as if someone had shouted his name in a language only he knew.

"Hold it," Alice called, but the dog was already there, quivering, tail thudding against the hard surface like a drum. The truck door shut outside. Another. Voices. One of them her boy's.

So excited anyone would think he'd been gone for years, not weeks. She wiped her hands on a towel and hurried to meet them. The knob turned and there Kade was, tall and sun-browned, grinning like he'd never left.

"Hi, Mom." Kade immediately dropped his duffel bag and closed the distance between the front door and his mother.

Grown son or not, he was still her boy. She threw her arms around him and squeezed hard, before stepping back to greet their guest. Looking up at the man, she extended her hand. "Welcome."

"This is Josh." Kade waved a thumb at his friend.

Alice squinted at him. "Welcome, Josh, Have we met?"

"You've heard me talk about him. We served together back in the days when Brady and I were a team."

"It's nice to meet you in person, Mrs. Sweet."

The pieces finally fell together and she reached out and pulled the guy into a big old bear hug. "I can't believe I finally get to meet you."

Brady, who'd happily been circling Kade's legs, waiting for his master's attention, suddenly froze. His nose twitched, and he turned his attention to Josh. The dog let out a soft whine, then bounded forward with such excitement that he nearly knocked Josh over.

"Whoa there!" Josh laughed, dropping to one knee as Brady circled him frantically, tail wagging so hard his whole body shook. "Hey buddy! You remember me, don't you?"

The dog pressed against Josh, licking his face and whining with pure joy.

"Nah, it's that hot dog you had for lunch," Kade teased.

"Now you know you are home." Alice patted the dog on the head. "Okay, Brady. Let the man catch his breath." The dog finally settled at her side, Alice waved for the boys to follow her. "Come on in, both of you. The cookies are warm, and I've got coffee ready."

Moving very slowly, Kade glanced around. "Cassie home?"

Alice couldn't help but smile. She loved the look in his eyes as he searched for his wife. Reminded her of his father.

"What's all the commo—" Cassie's mouth dropped open and she pretty much galloped down the stairs, flinging herself into Kade's open arms.

"There's a lot of that going on around here." She tipped her head toward the kitchen and gestured for Josh to follow her. "That hello might take a while."

"Yes, ma'am." Josh smiled, and like a good soldier, did what he was told.

"Have a seat. You want something hot or cold to drink?"

"Cold would be fine." He hadn't sat yet. "I can help myself."

She dipped her chin and finally nodded. "I suppose if Brady thinks you're family, then so do the rest of us. There's tea and lemonade in the fridge."

The man's eyes opened wide. "Fresh lemonade? The stuff that Kade spoke of as the elixir of the gods?"

That had her laughing. "I don't know about that, but

yes, fresh squeezed with a little strawberry too." For a second she thought, Josh might start to drool.

As Josh took a seat and eyed the fresh baked cookie bars, Kade and Cassie sauntered arm in arm into the kitchen, whispering softly to each other. Yep, her heart swelled at how happy her children were. Not that they weren't happy before when they were still single, but this was just a little different and made Alice's heart sing.

"Okay, everyone take a seat. I've got a pie cooling if anyone prefers a blueberry sour cream."

Josh let out a low moan, then immediately blushed. "Sorry ma'am, but Kade used to talk about you and your cooking so often, that we all wished we could teleport to Texas, but I never thought there'd be a day when I'd actually get to taste something you made."

"And that, young man, will get you an extra large slice." She smiled at him and patted his shoulder before indeed giving him a hefty hunk of her son's favorite pie.

Sitting down between his buddy and his wife, Kade glanced down at Brady lying at Josh's feet. "Traitor."

The dog twitched one ear and Alice would have bet the ranch that Brady shrugged a shoulder.

Ready to settle in and listen to the free-flowing banter between her son, his wife, and his friend, her phone buzzed with a message. She almost ignored it, but decided with all the chaos of the found money, the new cameras, and the search for Ray, she should at least check who it was. She immediately recognized the Florida area code. Brooklyn. *Trying to reach Clint, any idea where I can find him?*

When that man focused on a chore, a bomb could go off around him and he wouldn't flinch. "If y'all will excuse me a minute, I need to check on something in the barn."

Three heads nodded, but the conversation didn't slow.

She really missed having a full house. Heading out the back door, she moved toward the barn, pleased to find Benny mucking stalls. "How's it going?"

"Just fine, Ms. Sweet."

She looked around, craned her neck toward the tack room. "Any idea where Clint is?"

Benny shook his head. "No ma'am. He said he had something he'd been putting off too long, but didn't tell me what."

"I see. Thanks." What could he possibly have been putting off too long? Making her way back to the house, she considered the possibilities. For Brooklyn to reach out to her in search of Clint, he must really want to talk to her new foreman, but where to find him. She'd made it halfway to the main house when she spotted Clint pushing a wheel barrow across the yard, disappearing around the side of the house. Picking up her pace, she shifted trajectory to catch up with him. When she reached the side and found him dumping dirt, she stuttered to a halt. "What the heck?"

The only way to make a surprise stick on a place where ten people crossed the yard every five minutes would be to start in the middle of the night. That, unfortunately, had not been an option. Instead, taking a few hours early every morning, he'd managed to work quietly along the side of the house without drawing attention to himself. The trickiest part had been hauling the sand and compost from the opposite side of the house without anyone noticing. Until now.

The sound of Alice's voice held more curiosity than anger, but either way, he'd been busted before he was completely finished.

Her mouth hanging slightly open, her gaze darted left then right before meeting his. "You cleared out all the weeds."

Even though it was obvious, he nodded.

Immediately, her focus shifted to the piles of dirt and compost and sand to one side. Now she was taking inventory. The mountain of overgrown weeds and vines had been cleared, the weatherworn picket fence had been replaced with fresh treated wood, a swing gate with oiled hinges, and lined with chicken wire to keep hungry critters from munching.

Turning the soil for the beds was the last portion of this project. A few more hours and it would have been ready. "I'm almost finished."

"I don't know what to say."

He certainly hoped that was a good thing.

Shaking her head, she seemed to be searching for words. "You didn't lose the bet."

"No. But I figured it needed doing anyway. I mean if you were wanting to work the garden again it had to be done. Besides, homegrown always tastes better than store-bought."

"Yeah." She nodded. "That's why I was thinking it was time to clean this up."

"I hope you don't mind." It hadn't occurred to him that she might not want him to do this.

"Mind?" Finally, a smile teased at her lips. "I've been putting this off for months. Couldn't bring myself to even start. It was so… daunting."

He found that hard to believe. Alice Sweet wasn't the kind of woman to shirk hard work.

Bobbing her head, she seemed to be getting over her initial shock. Looking around, she spotted the pitchfork leaning against the wall. "All right. Let's finish this up. You shovel the soil and I'll turn it."

Now this was the Alice Sweet he'd come to know and respect. Ready to roll up her proverbial sleeves and do the hard work. "That won't be—"

Alice snapped her fingers and snapped erect. "I almost forgot why I came out here. Brooklyn has been trying to reach you."

Brooklyn. The name sent a jolt through him. The investigator had promised to call with updates on his case, but Clint hadn't expected to hear anything so soon. Reaching into his pocket, he pulled out his cell. Two missed calls. Not wasting another minute, he hit return call and listened to it ring.

"I'll just go back inside." Alice took a step in retreat and Clint reached out to grab her arm.

Shaking his head, he pulled his hand back, startled by

the unexpected jolt that had struck him. "Stay. This is all your doing. Besides, we have no secrets."

The phone rang twice before Brooklyn picked up. "Clint. I've been trying to reach you."

"Sorry. Ringer was off." He was tempted to dry his palms along his jeans, but didn't want Alice to misinterpret nervous energy for guilt. To ensure she knew he wasn't hiding anything, he put the phone on speaker.

"Been there, done that. I'm sorry it's taken this long to get back to you."

If he considered a week long, Clint wondered how fast did this man usually work?

"We've had a bit of a challenge gathering all the right information, but this morning we were able to reach your neighbor's wife. We think we have enough pieces of the puzzle to see more clearly."

Even though Brooklyn couldn't see, Clint nodded.

"The first thing we were able to discover about your neighbor is that Frank Walker liked to place bets. On anything. The ponies, auto racing, the weather, you name it. The problem, of course, like any addicted gambler, is that he lost—a lot. Dear Frank owed some *very* not nice people a *very* whole lot of money. Did you know his house was in foreclosure?"

His gaze drifted to Alice. "Recently I'd heard it sold in foreclosure, but I didn't know it back then."

"Well, he was scraping bottom. His wife had walked out on him by then. She confirmed all of this when we finally tracked her down."

"Does she know anything more?"

"No, but that was all we needed from her. You and Mrs. Sweet were correct in your suspicions that good old Frank didn't die from carbon monoxide poisoning. We got our people to take a second look at the autopsy report."

Clint waited for the other shoe to fall.

"There's this little thing called blunt force trauma. If the carbon monoxide didn't do him in, the fractured skull would have."

When had his life become nothing more than a bad

Hollywood movie?

"Here's where we've connected the dots but still need to dot our 'I's and cross our 'T's. If you keep in mind that your beat up blue pickup was in the driveway when you came home, and shortly thereafter your house is torched. Then remember that your neighbor also drove a similar blue pickup truck, even though not the same make, from a distance, say across the street. If a person is in a hurry, they may not realize the truck was a Ford not a Chevy."

Clint was doing his best to process all this info as fast as he could, and he wasn't liking how it was adding up. "Are you trying to say that I was a mistake?"

"I think so. From what we've learned from our sources, we've more or less pieced it all together. The loan shark wanted to make an example out of your neighbor. Instead, they torched the wrong house."

"Can you prove that?"

"Almost. Give us a few more days."

Clint almost choked on his own laughter. He'd waited all these years, would it kill him to wait a few more days?

CHAPTER TWELVE

Not since she was a young bride was Alice this excited about planting a few vegetables in her freshly cleared garden. Once she got over the shock of finding Clint working in what had been a jungle of overgrowth, and put aside the surprise of all Brooklyn had to report, she eagerly worked at his side to finish the prep work.

The thing that was even more unexpected than his clearing the space for no other reason than he remembered it was something she wanted to do, was how much she'd come to enjoy working at his side. And if she were honest with herself, dancing with the man. Everything about him was so... perfect. She knew there was no such thing as a perfect human, but danged if this man didn't come close. She had to laugh to herself. The way he rescued her stripped self, and fretted over her when she'd been hurt on the fence all those months ago, and stepped up to save a ranch that wasn't his—if ever there was a man worthy of a best-selling romance novel, Clint was it.

Of course, she had no business thinking of him as a hero, romantic or otherwise. For one thing, the man had to be a good ten years younger than her. And for another, she was his boss. Did thinking he'd make a perfect romantic hero qualify for sexual harassment? Of course not, at least not if it was just in her head. Maybe it was time she considered finding a new man. Maybe not to marry, but at least to go to a movie, or play a game of corn hole. Just... company. After all, it wouldn't be long before she'd be living in an empty house. *Empty house.* Dang, that sounded awful. It had been so much fun having Kade back and his buddy Josh. Watching those two horse around took her back twenty years to a house full of raucous teens. And she realized how much she'd missed that. Maybe it was time she told Sarah Sue that she was ready to start fostering dogs. Not the same as children, but she couldn't imagine life on this ranch without Brady.

"And what has you looking so distracted?" Clint appeared behind her. The tool belt clipped around his waist told her he had more work to do in her garden.

"Just contemplating the immortality of the crab."

A deep hearty laugh erupted as his head tipped back a moment. "I really love your approach to life."

She wondered if she was blushing, because she could feel heat rising from her toes to her cheeks. Straightening in place, her grip on the trowel tightened. "The only thing I'm approaching today is planting these seeds. What are you up to?"

His nose lifted toward the opposite side of the garden. "The old compost bin has seen better days. I just got back from town with fresh lumber. Was about to get started, but I can move on to something else if my hammering will bother you."

She shook her head. "I can't imagine a rancher in the world who the sound of hard work would disturb." Besides, she liked knowing he was near. Made no sense, but it was what it was.

She'd barely dug up the first few seed holes when Cassie came hurrying up beside her. "Sheriff Boyd is here."

"Here?"

"He said he was in the area and thought he'd stop by. Give you an update. Kade is inside with him and Carson is on his way over. Preston and Garret are tied up."

Nodding her head, Alice set her tools aside and peeled off her gloves, slapping them along a sideboard to shake loose the dirt before shoving them into her back pocket. Taking a single step, she paused and looked to Clint. "If this is about Ray, as our new foreman, you should probably come too."

His gaze leveled with hers and for a long moment he

remained silent. She knew he was debating whether or not that was his place and saw the moment he made up his mind, then he removed his tool belt, set it aside, and followed them into the house.

Inside, she followed the sounds of men's voices. Laughing voices. Well, that had to be a good sign. If something was truly wrong the tension should be thick as pea soup. Alice caught the tail end of some story about the sheriff catching Blake climbing in the window with Jillian holding a gun on him. Kade was laughing so hard, he was almost falling out of his seat. Of course, she knew that story, but Kade had been away and she guessed this was the first time he'd heard it.

As soon as they heard her cross the threshold, both men stood. Gotta love Texas chivalry. It made her right proud every time her sons or daughters did something, anything, to show her she and Charlie had raised them right. "Afternoon, sheriff."

"Miss Alice." He tipped his chin at her. No doubt if his hat had been on his head and not on the desk, he would have tipped it the way cowboys had done for generations before them.

"I hear you have news for me?" She waved for him to retake his seat.

Cassie moved to sit on the arm of the chair where her husband sat, and the sheriff plunked down in the comfortable easy chair at the same moment Carson came rushing into the room. "Got here as fast as I could."

"That wasn't necessary," the sheriff said. "I don't have much to report. Though we've caught two more of your former cohorts."

"Where?" she asked quickly.

"Millers Creek. They were drunk as skunks and spewing about being gypped out of a fortune. When they got around to telling a couple of working girls that they were going to get even and get their due share, one of them got nervous that they might be dangerous and the bartender called in the police."

"So Ray ripped them off too?" Carson asked.

"Looks like it. Unfortunately, the two lawyered up as soon as they sobered up. But we did learn that the reason they took off was because Ray got wind that you were going over the books. I guess he figured he needed to get out while the getting was good."

"Rats," Kade muttered.

"From what we gathered, he didn't dare take any of the money they'd accrued in case the law caught up with him. Same with the hands. He promised them if they lay low for six months, he'd give them their money when the heat was off."

"But he didn't?" Alice asked, even though it wasn't really a question.

The sheriff shrugged. "Doesn't look like it."

"So where does that leave us now?"

Clint stood along the back wall of what had once been Charles Sweet's office. If the hands were found so close to home, the hackles rising on the back of his neck told him that Ray might not be far behind. Unless, of course, he'd lied through his teeth and had taken more than enough money with him and, sure he was safe, was very long gone.

"One of the two let it slip that Ray had hidden the loot here on the ranch. But by then they'd sobered up enough to ask for a lawyer and shut their mouths."

"The hundred k we found?" Alice spoke softly.

Her voice was so low Clint almost didn't hear her. And yet, he had an overwhelming urge to cross the room and place a hand on her shoulder. A reminder that he was there if she needed him. That was the more acceptable behavior. What he really wanted was to hold her hand, squeeze it, reassure her, or better yet, wrap his arms around her and protect her from all this nasty business.

The sheriff nodded. "That's my guess."

Carson shook his head. "Except based on our math from the sold cattle, the sold equipment, lumber, etc., there has to be a helluva lot more money than that."

"You think he spent the rest?" Her spine straight again, Alice was frowning.

Marvelous. Now Clint wanted to run his thumb across the pleats in her forehead and make her worries go away. Clearly, he'd lost his mind.

"There has to be more somewhere." Kade pressed his lips tightly together and Cassie gently rubbed his shoulders.

"Cameras show anything?" the sheriff asked.

Both Kade and Carson shook their heads.

"I guess," Kade looked to his brother, "that would explain why we found remnants of someone digging."

"Either Ray was here looking for his loot, or one of the others."

"That doesn't make sense." Alice leaned forward. "I mean, maybe the hands, but not Ray. He'd have to know where he hid the money."

"Unless," the sheriff turned to face her, "he found it there and simply didn't have time to put things back the way he found them."

Alice shook her head. "Everything in me screams that whoever was digging, didn't find what they were looking for."

Clint's gut was telling him the same thing.

Hands on the arms of his chair, the sheriff pushed to his feet. "I do have some good news. With the four of your hands in custody, if we don't have a case against anyone, the DA will probably release your money in a few weeks."

"So he believes it's ours?" Carson asked.

Nodding, the sheriff reached for his hat. "Based on what those two yahoos said, yes, he believes it's most likely yours, but he still has to go through the process and bureaucracy is a lot of things, expedient ain't one of them."

No one moved, and Cassie hopped up from her perch on her husband's chair. "Let me walk you to the door, sheriff."

Smiling, the man nodded, and tipped his hat at Alice. "I'll reach out if we learn anything else from those yahoos."

"Thanks, sheriff."

He dipped his head in a silent your welcome and

followed Cassie out of the room.

"So," Kade's eyes narrowed, "who wants to bet if those two hands are back sniffing around, Ray can't be far."

Carson shook his head. "No point in borrowing trouble. For all we know, it was those hands who were digging for gold, so to speak, and not Ray."

"Well, I can't do much about it. Josh and I have to be back on base Monday morning."

"We can handle it." Carson nodded this time. "You protect the rest of the world. We'll watch out for the ranch."

Clint wanted to speak up, to reassure Kade that he was constantly vigilant and as of this minute, he was going to be much more vigilant. Especially where Alice Sweet was concerned. Ray might have gotten the better of the Sweets before, but he was not going to let that happen again anytime soon. Or ever.

"Do you think we need more cameras?" Alice asked. From what Clint could see, the question seemed to come more from a surveillance standpoint than from a position of fear.

Of course that made perfect sense. He'd yet to see Alice Sweet afraid of anything.

"With your permission, first thing in the morning, I'm going to head out to check more of the line shacks. See if there are any more hidden loot that we need to know about."

Carson nodded. "Except from now on, no one goes anywhere on this ranch alone. We'll do like dive buddies. Two or more."

"Agreed." Kade bobbed his head. "We are not to take any chances until Ray is caught and, preferably, behind bars."

"Do you think the two hands in custody will be released?"

"I hope not." Carson looked around the room. "I truly hope not."

Clint couldn't agree more. Not so much because he was afraid of the pipsqueaks, but more so because if he ever got his hands on the bastards who stole from Alice and made her and her family's lives so difficult, he couldn't promise he wouldn't wind up back in jail again, this time for a crime he *did* commit.

CHAPTER THIRTEEN

After several hours of pretending to be asleep, Alice decided that there was no such thing as fake it till you make it when it came to slumber. Climbing out of bed in the pitch of night was standard for ranchers. There was much to be done and the day always started early. For her, it was in the kitchen, but for the rest of the family or hands, the work was usually outdoors and always strenuous. Today, she would have a hearty breakfast ready for her crew and join Clint on his search of the shacks.

As soon as he'd mentioned checking for more stashes of cash or goods, she wondered why the heck hadn't they done that right away. It was foolish to assume that was the only money Ray or one of his people had hidden.

"Wow." Kade came into the kitchen with his buddy on his heel. "You're up early."

"I could say the same about you." She flipped pancakes on the griddle.

Josh chuckled. "She's got you there."

"What's your poison?" Alice pointed to the griddle. "Pancakes, there's a French toast casserole in the oven, eggs in the frying pan, and I've got bacon or sausage or both."

Her son's friend looked from the stove to Kade and back, and then, a smile took over his face. "I guess a little of everything."

"Keep eating like that and you're going to have to go on a crash diet before reporting back for duty."

"Hey," Josh raised his hands at Kade, "I'm no fool. Uncle Sam could learn a thing or two from your mother. I'm going to enjoy this home cooking for as long as I can."

The back door swung open. Removing his hat, Clint

slapped it against his thigh and stomped his boots on the mat.

"Hungry?" She waved a spatula at him.

"No, ma'am." He shook his head. "I've already eaten."

Swallowing quickly, Josh ran a napkin across his mouth. "You do not know what you're missing. You may want to rethink that."

Clint looked at Josh, gave a slow lazy smile and nodded. "Miss Alice is an excellent cook."

Now why did that little complement make her cheeks warm? "If you're not hungry, what brings you up to the house?"

"I've left Benny fixing the chute for vaccinating. Last time a few good kickers tore it up a bit and it needs to be reinforced before the next round."

Alice nodded. Having Benny around was helping them catch up on deferred maintenance.

"If you don't mind, I'm going to get an early start, check for some more loose floorboards in the shacks and make sure the cameras haven't been tampered with."

"Have a seat. I'm almost done with the last of the pancakes. Then I'll get my boots on and we'll go together."

"That won't be…" his voice dropped off at her glare. "Yes, ma'am."

She almost chuckled out loud. That look had worked just as well with all her children and Charlie too. It was kind of nice to know after all these years, she hadn't lost her touch.

From her husband's office, the door squeaking shut could be heard followed by the fall of booted heels against the floor. Carson came to a stop in the doorway. "I know we're ranchers, but isn't this rather early for everyone?"

"Couldn't sleep so I got up and started breakfast early." Alice shrugged.

"We were going to do a morning run, but we got waylaid by Mom's cooking." Kade shoveled a forkful of eggs into his mouth.

His mouth already full, Josh glanced up, smiled, and still chewing, nodded. The sight almost made Alice laugh.

She didn't care what their age was, she still saw little boys sitting at her table.

"Well, glad you're all up." She didn't like the look on Carson's face. "It may be nothing, but I was looking at the footage from the cameras, and I could have sworn I saw shadows in the distance along the back forty fence line."

Kade squinted, his forehead pleating with concentration. "That's pretty far to see from where the cameras are."

"I know," Carson said. "That's why I prefaced my observations with it could be nothing." His hand rubbed along the back of his neck. "Maybe I'm just paranoid with all the weird crap that keeps happening around here, but maybe—"

"Maybe," frowning, Clint leveled his gaze with Carson's, "someone is still messing with us. I'll check out the fence line first thing."

Alice flipped the last pancake, slid it onto an already-high stack and then put the dish in the oven. "If anyone wants more, they'll be warm in here."

All heads nodded, except Clint. "Maybe I should check this out alone."

Shaking her head, Alice caught herself in time to stop from rolling her eyes. "It will be daylight by the time we get to the back forty, I'm sure the boogeymen will be gone."

Though she knew he was still concerned, she spotted one corner of Clint's mouth tilting upward before he bit down on his back teeth and drew his lips into a thin line and nodded at her.

As if the man had ears in their kitchen, Alice's phone buzzed with a text from Brooklyn. *Call me when you're up.* That made her laugh. Apparently, the former SEAL had no idea about ranching hours. Quickly hitting the call button, she waited for him to pick up on the second ring. "Hi, Brooklyn."

"One of my men managed to get a lead on Ray."

Everyone stopped eating and looked up at her phone.

"From what we can tell, he holed up for a while working a few ranches in Wyoming, then Colorado, onto

Oklahoma, and now he's turned up in the panhandle."

"He's heading back," Kade muttered.

"That's our take," Brooklyn confirmed.

Alice tried to process the idea that Ray might be returning to the scene of the crime. Which told her two things: first, he probably had no idea they'd found his stash—at least one of them—and second, if that vermin ever set foot on this ranch again, she was still angry enough to kill the SOB with her bare hands. "Someone should tell Sheriff Brody."

"He's next on my list to call," Brooklyn told her. "In the meantime, keep an eye out. Do you need me to send a few men to help secure the property?"

Alice scanned the faces in the room. They all seemed to be thinking about it when Kade, after sharing a glance with Carson, sighed. "The man's a thief, he probably just wants to come back for his money and get out fast. We'll be fine."

Carson nodded.

Clint merely ground his teeth until the muscles at the base of his jaw twitched.

Yep. Right about now, no one was happy.

None of what he was hearing made Clint happy, but hopefully the family was right. Ray might be a crook without a conscience, but so far he hadn't proved dangerous. That didn't mean they had to sit back and do nothing.

"Come on." Alice slid into her boots and grabbed a jacket. "We've got a fence to check out and some line shacks to search. We'll bring Brady. If anyone is lurking, that dog will sniff him out even if he's upwind."

Clint nodded. What more could he do? She was his boss, not his wife. As much as he wanted to tell her to stay put, that he and Brady, or maybe even Benny too, would check things out. Unfortunately, though he was pretty sure it wouldn't be enough to get him fired, he also knew that it would go over about as well as a skunk in the kitchen.

Taking the four-wheeler to make better time, they pulled up to the section of fence where Carter thought he might have seen some movement where there shouldn't have been any cows. Hopping out, the two of them walked slowly along the fence line, carefully looking for anything out of the ordinary.

Walking ahead of Clint, Alice came to a sudden stop, squatted down on her haunches, and not touching anything, studied the ground in front of her.

"What did you find?" Clint squatted beside her, his gaze immediately falling on what Alice had seen. "Hmm."

"My thoughts exactly." She fingered the freshly turned dirt. "This section of fence was repaired months ago."

Clint nodded.

"Which means…"

"Someone must have dug these posts up and then put them back."

She cast a look over her shoulder toward the line shack not too far away. "We'd better check out the closest shack."

Not seeing any signs of recent travel by a vehicle or animals en route to the shack, Clint had to wonder why the heck would someone dig up and replace a pole? At the shack, just in case, he pulled the rifle from the rack and escorted Ms. Alice to the small space. Inside, he already knew what to do. Kicking the floorboards as he walked, he listened for a hollow sound. Nothing. This wasn't making sense. Why did they dig up the post over there? And who was responsible? Could the men from Millers Creek been the ones who ransacked the other building?

"What are you thinking?" Alice stood, hands on her hips, looking around, shaking her head.

"It doesn't make sense."

"Yeah, that's my thought too. We have to be missing something."

Bobbing his head, he turned and headed out the door, Alice on his heel. Walking slowly, he searched the perimeter.

"Over here." Alice crouched by the corner of the shack.

These old shacks were built a million years ago when pier and post foundations were used. By the trap door to access the plumbing under the cabin, the dirt had been moved.

"We should call the sheriff." Alice pushed to her feet, brushing off her hands and taking a step in retreat, tripped over a small rock and stumbled, her arms flapping like an injured bird.

Instantly, Clint lunged forward, his arms gripping hers. As the two tumbled to the ground, he rolled, his arms now wrapped tightly around her in a desperate effort to avoid squashing her beneath him. Successfully flipping them, he landed on his back—hard. His head bounced off the ground and Alice Sweet, all soft and pliable, was sprawled on top of him.

It took a minute for him to blink away the stars and open his eyes. Almost nose to nose, not even when they'd danced had he been this close to her. Eyes a sparkling deep shade of blue stared down at him. He could feel every thump of her rapid heartbeat against him. All rational thought flew out the window and sheer instinct kicked in. Tightening his hold with one arm, the other wrapped around her shoulder, closing the distance between them, his lips pressed against hers. Lips warm and smooth and sweet as honey had his brain rattled and his hormones in high gear.

Somewhere in the back of his addled mind he knew this was a serous mistake. He had no right. Then, the tiniest of moans reached what was left of his brain cells and it registered, she was kissing him back. All good sense—not that he had any at the moment—and all sense of propriety, flew out the window. He tightened his hold and kissed her again until he could barely breathe.

Just as suddenly as the urge to hold her close and kiss her long and hard had overtaken him, Alice suddenly froze in his arms and good sense smacked him upside the head. Letting his arms fall to his sides, he waited for her to inch back and right herself.

Pushing off of him and coming to her feet, she brushed her hands again, and took a careful step toward the side of the shack. "It looks like someone dragged something out from under." She sucked in a long deep breath and blew it out slowly. "Could have been a smaller piece of equipment but my money is on a backpack or sack of more cash."

Now standing, his mind was scrambling to keep up. Clearly she wasn't going to say anything about the kiss, which meant what? Was he to ignore it as well? Was she waiting for him to apologize? What the heck was he supposed to do now? Especially if he didn't want to lose the best job he'd ever had, and more importantly, being near Alice Sweet. "I, uh."

He barely got the sounds out before her hand flew up, palm out, and her head began to shake from side to side. "Don't. Lets focus on this. On Ray. On whatever it all means."

"Okay." He nodded and desperately tried to clear his mind. "I'll call the sheriff. There might be some prints left behind, though I doubt it."

"This probably explains the post. Whoever came out here wasn't in a vehicle, they were on foot."

"And they knew what they were looking for. Whoever found this stash, also put it here."

She nodded. "And our most likely candidate is—Ray."

"Ray," Clint echoed her words.

Now the question at hand was, is this it—or is he coming back for more?

CHAPTER FOURTEEN

ventually Alice would have to get a good night's sleep if she didn't want to fall asleep over the lunch table, she just didn't think that was going to happen any time soon. All she'd been able to think about since her stumble at the line shack yesterday was that soul-searing kiss. From Clint. She couldn't decide what had her more unsettled—the fact that she'd actually kissed him back, or that Charlie had never crossed her mind. Not even after she'd righted herself and her lips continued to tingle and her brain began to unrattle, Charlie was nowhere in her thoughts. Heck, he hadn't made an appearance until she walked past her old master bedroom door and almost collapsed from the reminder that she was a married woman—sort of.

Kade and Josh made their way into the kitchen from upstairs. "You all packed?" she asked.

"Uh," Kade looked to Josh then back to his mother, "not exactly."

"Then you still have time?"

"Definitely." Josh nodded with a smile at the same time Kade flashed his buddy a stern, almost scolding look.

Focusing on his mother, Kade smiled more widely. "I have a little surprise for you too."

"Okay…" She could use a good surprise right about now. Especially if it could keep her distracted from her own thoughts.

"We've got a whole week off." Her son beamed.

"A week off?"

"For good behavior." Kade nodded. His buddy rolled his eyes.

"Since when does the military give extra time off?"

Her son struggled to offer a casual shrug. Josh had developed a sudden interest in a non-existent piece of lint on his jeans.

"All right." She crossed her arms. "Spit it out. What's going on?"

"Well," Kade ran a hand across the back of his neck, "I may have explained to my CO that there's a serious threat at the ranch, and that my widowed mother is home alone all day."

"And that worked?" She let her arms fall to her sides.

His arm still hanging from behind his neck, Kade chuckled. "Yeah, surprised the hell out of me too."

Just then the back door opened and in walked Clint—the reason she'd barely gotten any sleep at all last night.

"Morning." He held his hat in his hands. "I, uh, thought I'd check in before heading back out to work. Do, uh, you need anything?"

Her tongue seemed stuck to the roof of her mouth so she settled for a shake of her head. At that moment, Clint's phone dinged with a text. He glanced down, frowned, and slid it back into his pocket.

"Something wrong?" she asked.

Clint shook his head. "Nothing serious."

"Is it about, you know, the fire?"

"No." Clint seemed to relax at her question.

Had he been having as rough a time of it as she was? Somehow she was going to have to find the strength to talk to this man without sounding like a babbling idiot. But now with an audience wasn't going to be the time.

"I'd better get back to work." He cast a glance in the boys' direction. "If you two are looking for something to keep you out of trouble, I never turn down a helping hand."

The two looked at each other a moment, seemed to have some silent communication, almost like an old married couple—though Alice suspected in many ways military teams were indeed like old married couples when it came to having each other's backs—and then stood straight. "We're all yours," Kade offered.

Clint placed his hat on his head, and dipped his chin at her. "You let me know if the sheriff has anything else to say."

She figured if communication was going to happen, now would be a good time to put everyone at ease. Sucking in a deep breath, she flashed the brightest smile she could muster. "I will."

Was it wrong of her to wish the sheriff would call sooner than later so she'd have a chance to hear that deep timbre again?

The back door snapped shut as the three men strode away from the house. Clint's mind had been reeling from yesterday's kiss with Alice. If he'd gotten any sleep last night, he hadn't noticed. But at the moment, whatever he was feeling needed to be pushed aside.

"So what's really going on?" Kade matched Clint's quick stride.

Clint glanced over his shoulder, making sure they were out of earshot of the house. "Text was from Carson. His phone's going crazy with alerts. Security cameras picked up a truck parked by the east pasture line shack and two guys making more noise than a high school brass band."

"And you didn't tell Mom because…?" Kade's voice held more curiosity than accusation.

"Your brother didn't want her anywhere near this. Said to grab you two if you were available. We all know if she heard, she'd be storming off beside us."

"Mom is a bit of a pistol," Kade said. "She's also tough and smart."

Didn't he know that? "So you want her to come?"

"I didn't say that." Kade sighed. "But I want it on record, she's not a delicate flower that will shrivel with the first cold wind."

On that, Clint could easily agree, but he also knew he didn't want Alice anywhere near that shack, especially if

Ray and his buddies were up to no good.

"For what it's worth, I'm with Carson. I like your mom too much to put her at risk." Josh shrugged. "Just lead the way."

Clint veered right, heading toward the bunkhouse instead of the barn. "We should grab some firepower. Better to have it and not need it…"

"Than need it and not have it," Kade finished, following Clint up the bunkhouse steps. At the door, Clint threw the bolt, stepped into the dim cool, and went straight to the locker where the long guns lived. Habit made the rest easy: check clear, magazines, chamber, sling. He passed one across to Kade, another to Josh, kept the third.

"I worked with Ray a short while before he took off. I wouldn't have thought him dangerous back then, but now, knowing all I do…" He didn't have to say anything else. Both men understood and nodded their agreement. The men handled the weaponry like old friends. No talk. No drama. Just done. They definitely understood.

Rifles in hand, they exited the bunk house and climbed into the waiting truck. The engine roared to life and they drove faster than they probably should have toward where Carson had said all the activity was.

"So," Kade broke the silence as they bumped along a rutted trail, "do we have a plan?"

"Hard to plan when you don't know what you're up against." Clint focused on the land ahead. "We'll park behind that rise. Approach on foot from there."

Ten minutes later, they crested the small hill overlooking the east pasture. Sure enough, a beat-up old truck was parked, engines running, a few feet from the shack.

"I count two," Josh murmured, his military training evident in his posture. "One inside, one out back."

Clint nodded. "We'll circle around. Kade, you take the south approach. Josh, east. I'll come in from the north." The three men separated, moving with practiced stealth toward the small structure. Closer now, Clint could hear voices— agitated, impatient.

"Ray sure as hell better show up soon," this came from a face he didn't recognize.

"He knows what he's doing," came the reply from inside, the voice familiar, but Clint couldn't place it. "Besides, we'll have plenty of time."

Clint caught Kade's eye across the clearing, giving him a slight nod. They moved in closer, weapons ready.

A loud crash came from inside the shack, followed by colorful cursing. "Damn it, would you be careful? You're making enough noise to wake the dead!"

"I thought that was the idea."

"No, you idiot. We're just supposed to keep the cameras busy, then as soon as Ray gets here, we're gone."

"And we'll be richer than a small country."

So they were right. Ray was on his way back, but why did he need these yahoos to keep the cameras busy? That part made no sense.

Clint signaled to the others, holding up three fingers. Two. One.

No longer trying to hide their approach, while Kade carefully opened a rear window to the single-room shack, rifle raised and ready, Josh covering him, Clint stomped up the two steps.

"About time you got here. If we didn't like you, we'd be halfway to Mexico by now." A bag in each hand, the man straightened and turned, his eyes popping wide, staring at the long end of a rifle. "Whoa, we'll share."

Share? Clint placed the voice now. He'd only met the guy a few times, a friend of Ray's. "Hands where I can see them!"

The other guy spun, only to find Kade pointing a rifle at him from the other side of the window. "Go ahead. Make my day."

"Ooh," Josh chuckled, "I've always wanted to say that."

The guy Clint didn't recognize took a brazen step forward.

Clint slid his finger onto the trigger shaking his head, but Josh was the one, still smiling, who said, "I wouldn't do that if I were you."

The two men glanced at each other and the hairs on the back of his neck stood upright. "Who are you waiting for? Who did you think we were?"

Again, the two men exchanged glances, but neither spoke.

"You know," Kade sighed, "my finger is getting tired. It would be really easy to slip and fire off a bullet. How do you feel about your family jewels?"

"You can't do that. We're not armed."

His weapon still trained on the two bungling burglars, Josh turned to Kade. "Are we police?"

Kade shook his head.

"Texas is a castle law state, right? We can shoot anyone trespassing?"

Both Kade and Clint nodded.

Josh, on the other hand, smiled wider. "Then I guess he can. Shoot you, that is." Not waiting for instruction, Josh grabbed a coil of rope hanging from a screw on the wall and quickly got to hog-tying the one guy.

Kade blinked. "Where'd you learn to do that?"

"I'll tell you later." Josh chuckled under his breath. "Don't you have more important things to deal with?"

"Right." Kade focused on the other guy still standing there with his hands in the air. "Who were you expecting?"

After a quick glance at his buddy tied up like a calf at a rodeo, he sighed. "Ray's supposed to be here."

Working as quickly as he had with the first intruder, Josh twisted the guy's arms behind his back and made fast work of tying them.

"When?" Clint uttered.

The guy shrugged. "He said he had some business to attend to and would meet us here."

Shoving the man over by his buddy, in no time, Josh had him tied up nice and neat.

Business. Here. Make noise. The dots connected for Clint and the others at the same time, as all three shouted, "The house!"

"Go." Josh pointed to the door. "These characters aren't going anywhere."

Running full speed ahead like a fox chased by a pack of hounds, Clint took off for the truck. All he could think was he'd left Alice alone. What had he been thinking?

CHAPTER FIFTEEN

Something didn't feel right, but Alice couldn't put her finger on it. The house felt…odd. Quiet. Too quiet. She couldn't remember the last time she'd been alone in this old house. Kade and his friend had gone to help Clint, Carson and Jess were at work, Mason at school, Cassie was helping Jillian sort through a large order at the candle shop, and even Brady was nowhere to be seen. Probably off with Benny or the others. She should have appreciated a little true peace and quiet, but instead she felt nervous, edgy, and she doubted it had anything to do with why she'd had so much trouble sleeping last night.

Emptying the last of the clean silverware from the dishwasher, the back screen gave a soft, uncertain squeak. Alice didn't turn right away. Doors breathed all day on a ranch—wind, kids, dogs, life, and yet, she found herself reaching for her phone on the counter. Maybe a quick call to Clint would settle this uneasy feeling.

"I wouldn't do that if I were you."

She didn't have to turn to see who the voice belonged to. She'd heard it day in and day out for too many years. Her hand only inches from the phone, she heaved a deep sigh and didn't bother to turn around. "Ray."

"Good morning, Mrs. Sweet. Hope I'm not interrupting anything."

"Morning." She straightened her shoulders and slowly turned. "You're trespassing."

He smiled like she'd told a joke he didn't mind. "I'm visiting."

"Unexpected guests bring pie." She kept her hands where he could see them. And because good manners were free, and she could use a little time for the boys to come back, she forced a smile. "Coffee?"

"Later." His gaze slid past her toward the hall. "Safe's still in the office?"

"What does it matter to you?" She lifted her chin in defiance.

"You know damn well what I want. I want my hundred k that you confiscated."

"Why would I have your money?"

His wry smile turned to a sneer. "You and that stupid ex-con. I thought for sure he'd fit right in with my crew. Turned out to be the most honest convict on the planet. He was so fastidious in caring for this place as if it were his own, just about drove the rest of us nuts."

At least her faith in Clint had just been confirmed. Not that she needed the confirmation of this conniving crook, but it was still nice to hear.

"I saw you."

Her heart, already hammering at twice its normal beat, now kicked it up another notch. How could they not have known he'd been here, watching?

"Everybody running around like they'd found the motherlode. And that fat sheriff. Puffing his chest like a damn peacock. Man couldn't find his own fingers if they were in front of his face."

She did not like the look in his eyes. Had they always been so sinister?

Suddenly, he barked out an almost maniacal laugh. "You haven't a clue, do you? You still haven't figured it out. Y'all were so busy placing new cameras trying to track us, it never occurred to a single one of you that I might have cameras watching you?"

Despite the shock, she tried to keep her expression neutral. The way he kicked his head back and laughed again, she'd probably failed.

"I know everything you've been up to." He shook his head. "How would dear Charlie feel about his wife cavorting with the hired help?"

If she'd been even a little afraid of him, now she was

simply furious. How dare he? It took every ounce of self-control she possessed not to lash out at him, but she was not stupid. She was nowhere near the gun cabinet and the man had over fifty pounds of muscle on her. There had to be a way to subdue him until someone came back.

"I want my money," he spat, all humor gone from his eyes.

"I don't have your money."

"Not all of it. Just a hundred grand of it and I want it." His right hand reached under his jacket and reappeared with a semi-automatic gun. "And I want it now."

"If you were watching, you'd know the sheriff took the money. Evidence."

"Do you think I'm stupid? There's no case. With no case you don't need evidence. I want my money. Ecuador is calling my name."

"Ecuador?"

"It's a country in South America."

"I know where Ecuador is."

"Oh yeah." That sneer was back. "The almighty Alice Sweet is so smart. Did you know Ecuador has no extradition treaty with the US?"

"Why would I know that? I'm not a criminal."

"No. You're just Mrs. Charles Sweet, upstanding citizen, legacy rancher. Your family has no idea how hard it is for a working man to save for a spread of his own. Every time you've got enough money, the cost of the land goes up and you start all over again. Over and over, year after year."

Different responses bounced around in her head. The question at hand, which response wouldn't fuel his anger with the Sweet family, with her. At that moment, as she struggled for something to say, the right thing to say, her phone rang. Only inches out of reach, she took a chance and stepped to the side, closer to the phone.

"Don't even think about it." Now he was waving a loaded gun in her direction. What a holy mess.

The phone stopped and she dared to take a half step in retreat. A half step closer to her phone.

"My money," he repeated. "Then I'll be on my way to

Mexico and then a flight to Ecuador."

"I told you, I do not have it. The sheriff does."

Fury fired in his eyes again. "March!" He waved the gun from her to the hall.

Her gaze darted to the phone. No way she could snatch it up without his seeing or without getting shot. Same with her gun. But did she have a choice? She must have been staring in the wrong direction too long because in a flash, a bang deafened her and a bullet flew past her, lodging in the wall behind her.

"I want my money."

He must have left the back door ajar because she could see it easing open, very slowly. Any hopes of a someone coming to her rescue were dashed when the door was fully open and no one appeared until her gaze dropped to the ground. Crawling like a plumber under an old house hunting down a leak, Brady was ever so slowly and quietly inching forward. It had never occurred to her that if Brady had been in the house, his military training would kick in.

Before she could react, Ray turned in the direction she'd been looking. His whole body turned and arm held straight out, he pointed his firearm at her precious Brady. "No!" ripped from her lungs as she lunged forward, throwing herself low in hopes of knocking him off his feet before he could pull the trigger.

Slamming hard on the floor, she held her arms forward and shoved at the back of his knees with all her might, the sound of another shot echoing loudly in her ears. All she could think was not Brady. Dear lord, not Brady.

"Come on, Mom. Answer." Phone to his ear, Kade spat through clenched teeth.

His own phone in front of him as they all ran to the truck, Clint called Benny's cell, each ring taking an eternity until finally the kid answered. "Hello."

"Where are you?" Clint hopped into the truck, turning

the engine as the others climbed in.

"Replacing the well pump. Remember?"

Damn it. "Yeah, yeah." He'd forgotten that Benny wasn't working in the barn today.

"What do you need?"

Running calculations in his mind, even if Benny flew like the wind, Clint and the guys had a more likely chance of reaching the house first by a wide margin. Still, this was Alice he was worried about. "There may be trouble at the house. Drop everything and get back as fast as you can."

"Yes, sir."

"And Benny?"

"Yes."

"You'd better bring your rifle."

The kid breathed for a second before saying, "Got it. I'll hurry."

There was no need to say anything else. The kid had been raised on ranches his whole life, he knew that anything could happen and he clearly understood that Miss Alice could be in trouble.

"Don't worry about speed limits," Kade ground out.

"That's the plan." The truck sailed across the fields and pastures faster than Clint had ever driven. Several times the rear end of the vehicle went airborne as he flew over a rut or mound. No one said a word. None of it mattered. Bruises would heal. Not so much Alice if Ray was really at the house.

As they approached the house, from a distance everything looked deceptively normal. What should have calmed his frayed nerves only increased the acid churning in his gut. Clint didn't take his eyes off the house ahead. "Try her again."

Without a word, Kade had the phone to his ear again.

Josh leaned forward from the back seat. "Can't we go any faster?"

"It won't do her any good if we flip this sucker over and break our necks." But he too wished he could go faster.

The sound of a gunshot cracked through the air, clear even at this distance.

"Jesus," Kade uttered, his face draining of color.

Clint's knuckles went white on the steering wheel as he pushed the truck faster across the uneven ground. Horrible visions of Alice lying on the floor in a pool of blood, the life draining out of her, flashed before his eyes. More ugly thoughts of Alice injured, in pain, with Ray taking advantage of an empty house and no hands around. Both visions had him hitting the accelerator even harder.

No sooner had the truck skidded to a halt by the back porch then the three of them leapt from the vehicle, greeted by Alice's voice screaming loudly *NO* accompanied by another gunshot. Never had his heart hammered so violently in his chest. Not even when he battled the heat and smoke in a failed effort to save his wife, not even then had he been as terrified of what he'd find as he was at this very minute.

Taking the porch steps two at a time, he was only steps ahead of Kade and Josh. Crashes and thuds and groans carried from the open door. Heaven help Ray if he'd hurt even one hair on Alice's head, Kade and Josh would have to wait their turn. Clint would easily beat the man within an inch of his life. With no idea of what he'd find, he held his finger to his lips and took the lead, slowly, quietly inching the already ajar door fully open, rifle in his hand, prepared to shoot to kill if necessary.

Only the sight ahead had him stuttering to a stop, Kade and Josh nearly plowed into his back.

Standing over Ray's prone body, a string of clothesline dangling from her hands, Alice tore her gaze away from the man out cold on the floor and leveled her eyes with Clint's. "He was going to shoot Brady."

At Ray's feet, teeth exposed under a steady snarl, Brady was poised to take over if the man stirred. To the side of Ray's head, a cast iron frying pan lay on the floor.

"I couldn't reach my gun, but after I knocked him to the ground, the frying pan was within reach." Alice shrugged. "I'm not sure if he's even breathing, but I figured better to tie him up first and determine if he's alive or dead later."

Kade stepped up to his mother, and kissed her temple. "Nice work."

"Allow me." Josh relieved Alice of the thin rope, then squatted and put two fingers to Ray's neck. "I'm sorry to report he's still breathing."

Sirens could be heard shattering the eerie quiet. By the time Josh had Ray's hands tightly bound, with Clint's rifle trained on their former foreman, the man began to groan and writhe.

"I wouldn't move if I were you." Josh actually smiled at the guy. "I don't think you want to piss off Mrs. Sweet again."

The front door burst open, and weapon drawn, Sheriff Boyd came through the house, stopping at the kitchen entry. "Well," he holstered his gun, "looks like you folks had quite a day."

Alice nodded. "He came for his money. Said he was heading to Ecuador."

"Not anymore, he's not," Boyd replied, kneeling to check Ray's bindings. "Nice knot work."

Josh shrugged.

Leaning into his friend, Kade whispered out of the side of his mouth. "Where *did* you learn to do that?"

Biting back a grin, Josh looked at his buddy, his words barely audible. "Might have something to do with a trick rodeo roper I briefly...uh, dated."

A burst of laughter erupted from Kade. "Not touching that one with a ten-foot pole."

Shaking his head, Clint seemed to be the only one who noticed the friends' quiet exchange.

As soon as the deputy arrived to assist the sheriff, and Ray was securely cuffed and loaded into the ambulance, Alice seemed to deflate, all the fight and fear leaving her at once. Her hands shaking, Clint inched closer. The minute all the cars drove off, she turned and nearly collapsed against him. Her face pressed into his shoulder, his arms went around her automatically, one hand cradling the back of her head. "It's okay," he murmured into her hair. "You did good. It's okay now."

Heaving in deep breaths, Alice remained against him as he drew slow lazy circles across her back. "Thank you."

Slowly, she inched back, blew out one long breath, and nodded as if reassuring herself she was indeed all right. "I guess it's over. Really over."

Reluctantly, Clint let his arms fall to his side, letting her decide, now that the adrenaline rush was over, where she wanted to be. "There's more money. They were gathering it up from where Ray had stashed a lot of it around the ranch. It should help a great deal."

Still standing close enough that he could easily put his arms around her again if he were willing to risk it, she glanced up at him. "I'm going to guess there's more of it in a bank account in Ecuador."

"Makes sense. Probably crossed the border into Mexico by car, not a whole lot of records coming and going that way, then flew to Ecuador."

Taking a surprising step forward, Alice let her head fall against his shoulder again. "I don't care if he went to Antarctica, I'm just glad I'll never have to see him again."

Hesitant, unsure, Clint finally lifted his arm around her, first one, then the other. When she was fully in his embrace, she tipped her hand and glanced up. "I think we're going to be okay now."

He nodded.

"Both of us."

Now he wasn't so sure if he was following her drift, or if it was merely wishful thinking. Raising one brow, he didn't say a word, just waited.

A smile bloomed across her lips. "Well, cowboy. Aren't you going to kiss me?"

"Yes, ma'am."

Two throats cleared, and in the background he heard Kade mutter to his friend, "I think we're not needed here anymore."

CHAPTER SIXTEEN

Every morning, for the last few weeks, Alice felt like pinching herself. She'd gone from a tired widow dealing with criminals, financial threats, deferred maintenance, downed fences, and restoring line shacks, to functionality. Now, they had recovered enough money to repay the loans, and start work on Carson and Jess's house. Their new home would be close enough to visit, far enough for privacy. But the biggest change had been Clint. He'd gone from a reliable hand, to a trusted friend and foreman, to her anchor.

When Charlie died, it never occurred to Alice that she would ever love or want again. She'd lost her best friend and confidant of over thirty years and couldn't fathom anyone ever filling those treasured shoes. Then, just like that, she couldn't imagine her life without Clint in it.

The coffee was on, the eggs were in the warming oven, and she was in the process of turning the bacon as Cassie came down the stairs. "Oh, that coffee never smelled so good."

"Toast?"

"I'll fix it." Breathing in the coffee aroma as if it were smelling salts, Cassie smiled and opened the bag of bread.

Footsteps smacked against the wooden stairs. Carson appearing a moment later.

"You're up awfully early." Now that they had a full staff of hired hands, her kids no longer had to suffer through two jobs, though Cassie liked working the ranch and opted to learn everything she could rather than going back to school—at least for now.

Standing at the beloved coffee pot, he nodded. "Filling

in for the coach this morning. Early practice. Too early if you ask me.”

The back door eased open and Clint came inside. Hanging his hat on the hook and stomping his boots on the mat, his entire stance was relaxed and easy. “Morning’”

Without asking, Carson filled another mug and handed it to Clint. By now they all knew he drank it black no sugar.

“Thanks.” Smiling at Alice, the warmth in his eyes gave her goose bumps as though she were a teen being noticed by the captain of the football team.

Within minutes, everyone was seated at the table, food overflowing, conversation easy. There was no longer foreman and employers but ranchers with the same goal—uplifting the Sweet Ranch.

“I got a call from Sean Farraday last night.”

“Really?” Alice took a sip of her juice. “What was he wanting?”

“An update on Ray. I told him that the district attorney assured us there isn’t a snowball’s chance in hell that he’s going to walk away from this. Same for the two idiots we caught with him.”

“Sounds like all the culprits are now where they belong.” Carson stabbed at his eggs. “Behind bars.”

“For a good long time,” Cassie said with a satisfied grin. The woman hadn’t been a Sweet family member for long, but she had family loyalty running in every vein of her body.

“As you know, his son Connor owns one of the best horse breeding ranches in the country.”

Alice nodded.

“It reminded me of something Preston said not long ago.” He set his gaze on Alice. “Charlie used to talk about breeding horses.”

“That’s right. I think after he updated the barns and all the other bases for the ranch, he wanted to expand.”

Clint toyed with his eggs. “I think we’re in a place where we can do that. What Charlie planned. If you’d like.”

If she didn’t already know that she loved Clint Gibbons, she would have figured it out right about now. The man was amazing. Honoring Charlie, loving her, caring for this ranch as if he too had been born to it. And never ever overstepping.

"I think it's a great idea. If you're sure, we can handle it."

He nodded, turned to Carson. "And you."

"I'm all for it." Carson pushed away from the table. "I have to run. You guys let me know when we start the horse business."

Another few minutes of finishing up breakfast and Clint and Alice were the only two left in the kitchen. Even though it wasn't his job in any way shape or form, they had fallen into a routine. Clint joined them every day for meals, and when the family scattered after breakfast, they cleaned the kitchen together.

She'd washed and he dried the large pans she didn't like putting in the dishwasher, the whole time wondering if she'd overstepped her limits, if she'd gone too far in her surprise. Shortly after Ray was in custody, Brooklyn had reached out to them again. One of his people had tracked down the neighbors on the opposite side of Clint's former house, Mr. and Mrs. Jerry Baxter, and learned that a black truck had been parked in front of the house most of the day. Coming and going. Mrs. Baxter had actually written down the license plate just in case any of the neighbors turned up burglarized.

When Clint asked if she'd told the police, Brooklyn had sighed heavily, telling them that she didn't report it. And when asked why, she easily said, they didn't ask me.

It took Alice a long while and two glasses of wine to get over her fury at the woman's nonchalance. Her neighbor's home burned to the ground and the owner accused of murder and it never dawned on her to report what she'd seen. It had also helped appease her fury when Brooklyn explained that because of this, they were able to confirm their suspicions. The people his neighbor owed money to had indeed burned down the wrong house. Soon Clint would be officially cleared, and a nice fat check was coming his way for wrongful imprisonment. Not that it could come close to undoing the mess it had made of his life and relationship with his son.

She'd tried to talk Clint into calling Jason, but he'd shake his head and say not yet, he needs time to adjust, to decide if he wants me in his life again. Dutifully, she said nothing more. It struck her that perhaps they were both going to need time. Until she got the call. It was Jillian. She'd driven to Midland to meet the plane. *ETA five minutes.*

Five more minutes and she'd either be on top of the world or in the dog house and she had no idea which of the two it would be.

"Something wrong?" Clint continued to wipe the pans dry.

"No, not at all." Her smile was as beautiful as ever, but shaky. Heaving a deep sigh, she turned off the water and turned, leaning a hip against the counter. "I did something and now I'm not sure it was the right thing to do."

Still drying a pan that was already dry, he nodded. "Does this something have anything to do with me?"

She nodded.

His heart suddenly felt like it had been placed in a vise. At first, it had been hard for him to accept that life could be so good for him. That Alice was his and that they had a future. Now, all of this new world had begun to feel very normal to him. None of her kids seemed to mind. As a matter of fact, they all seemed to like him well enough. None of the hired hands knew anything different than he and Alice had become a team, but now, those words *I'm not sure I did the right thing* had his insides twisting painfully. "Want to tell me about it?"

The one thing he'd come to appreciate more than he expected was how they talked over everything. It was so very different than his relationship with his late wife. As far as he knew, so far they had no secrets from each other. Hell, she knew the worst of his. And frankly, he doubted she ever had a real secret in her life, but still, he thought he knew everything about her.

The sound of tires crunching gravel carried through the house and Alice straightened her shoulders. "I'm afraid I'm out of time. I should have told you. I'm sorry. Remember that." She pushed away from the sink and strode across the living room to open the door.

What the heck was going on? Jillian was first in the door. She gave her mom a hug and a smile and a short nod. At least to Jillian, whatever this surprise was, it wasn't a bad thing.

The next person through the door was a tall young man, broad-shouldered, in khakis and a button-down shirt with dark leather loafers. A city dude. "Mrs. Sweet, thank you for having me."

"Please call me Alice."

"Yes, ma'am."

Alice chuckled. At least whoever the guy was, he had manners. It took another second for the visitor to step aside and fully face Clint. In that one single moment, he knew. The face of a scared little boy flashed before his eyes. Only now that face was a polite grown man who looked just as nervous as Clint suddenly felt.

Alice came out from behind Jason. "Come sit." She waved him toward the living room sofa, but the kid didn't move. His gaze was fixed on Clint. "Well, then." Alice moved toward Clint, stopping in front of him, her hand resting on his forearm. "Brooklyn called me yesterday, said he'd explained everything to Jason. Told me he wanted to see you. I overstepped and said that would be great. I got a text last night that he was arriving in Midland on the red-eye. I guess he didn't want to wait."

Forcing himself to look away from his son, he looked into Alice's eyes, eyes filled with fear, and made himself smile.

"I was afraid if I told you that you would just worry yourself all night and probably not sleep."

Now he chuckled. "So instead, you worried yourself all night and didn't sleep."

Her smile reappeared. "Something like that. I'll go make tea."

Jillian followed her mother into the kitchen and Clint cautiously moved closer to his son. "It's good to see you."

Jason didn't move. "I wasn't sure you'd want me to come."

"What?" Clint blinked, fear overshadowed by confusion. "Not want you?"

That scared little boy reared his head and Jason glanced at the floor before returning his attention to his father. "I should have believed you. I should have known."

Shaking his head, Clint closed the gap and instinctively pulled his son into his arms. "It's not your fault. The evidence was heavy. You were just a little boy."

"Still." His arms tightened around Clint. "I'm so sorry, Dad."

Dad. He never thought he'd hear that word again. "It's okay. Really. I'm the one who's sorry I couldn't be there for you all these years. I'm sorry I couldn't make your mother happy. Sorry I moved us next door to that idiot neighbor. Sorry for so many things."

The two hung onto each other for a long few minutes before Clint finally eased back. "Have you eaten?"

Jason shook his head.

"I just happen to know the best cook in West Texas and I bet I can get her to rustle you up something delicious to eat."

From the kitchen, Alice shouted over her shoulder. "I'm already on it. Come in here and take a seat." She waved a spatula at them. "And I want to hear all about your life."

"Yes, ma'am." Jason smiled.

His arm draped around his son's shoulder, they walked into the kitchen. What had he ever done to deserve Alice Sweet?

EPILOGUE

"**I** see what you mean." Josh chuckled at his buddy. "I always thought your description of a barn dance was creative exaggeration."

Kade smiled. "Is that like literary license?"

"Something like that." He'd been watching all the Sweet family siblings. If anyone had told him that six out of six siblings were happily married and obviously so to anyone watching, even if the couple were across the room from each other, Josh would have said that it was statistically impossible. So much for math.

"How are you enjoying a good old-fashioned barn dance?" Jillian came up to Josh. She was the one married to the country music star.

By now he was pretty sure he had who was married to whom down. Of course, he'd known all the siblings. Years of working side by side with Kade, he almost felt like he was part of the same family. "It's everything Kade said it would be."

He still wasn't sure what they were celebrating, but he was truly happy that he was still stateside to join Kade for the fun. He was especially happy to see how well things had worked out for Kade's mother and Clint. When he'd first learned of Charlie Sweet's unexpected death, he'd ached for the whole family, especially knowing how close they all were. Everyone loved their parents, and everyone had stories of clashes with parents, but Kade made it sound like they all grew up in a fairytale and their father and mother were Prince Charming and his beloved Princess. Never having met them in person, it still broke his heart learning of Charlie's death, and worrying about Alice Sweet alongside her son.

The band shifted to some country tune he wasn't truly familiar with and the crowd parted like the Red Sea. At the center of the dance floor, Alice and Clint were doing a mean two-step. Not the walking shuffle that he'd seen at too many wannabe country western bars, but the walking step with turns and spins and they looked like professional dancers—or old married people who had been dancing together for most of their lives. Of course, they were neither, but he strongly suspected, some day not too far away, they would become one of those old married couples.

"Kind of sweet, no pun intended, isn't it?" Sarah Sue, Preston's wife, came and sat beside him. "I just love seeing them together. I mean, it was a bit of a shock at first, but if they will be half as happy as she and Mr. Sweet were, they will be one blessed couple."

"That's what Kade said." Maybe it was something in the Texas water. There seemed to be an awful lot of happy around here and not much melodrama to go with it. Frankly, it wasn't normal. It was almost worrisome. Not quite as bad as Stepford, but so perfect that he found himself for the first time in a long time, tempted to hang up his military career and settle down. And how stupid was that?

"And what are you two whispering about?" Preston came and set a glass of lemonade in front of his wife. Kissed her firmly, yet discreetly, on the lips, then slung his leg over the chair and took a seat, his hands hanging off the back as he watched his mother dance.

More people joined on the floor and when the song was over, Alice and Clint made their way back to the table, not fully holding hands like besotted teens, but just a few fingers linked, as if they couldn't quite bear not being connected. There was little doubt in Josh's mind that there would be another wedding coming—sooner than later. Of course, he doubted he'd be on the guest list, but regardless, he was very happy for his current hostess.

Alice flopped into the seat opposite Josh, her hand fanning her neck. "Okay, I am seriously out of shape."

Merely raising a brow, Clint, ever the gentleman, said

nothing as he sat beside her.

Sarah Sue stood from her seat and moved around to sit next to Alice. "Since we have a few minutes, I need to know if you were serious when you said you might like to take on fostering K9s?"

"Oh." Alice looked to Clint, who merely smiled at her when Josh realized, the lingering look wasn't lust but communication. The two had not said a single word, only a hint of a smile, a slight lift of a brow, tip of the head and then Alice Sweet turned to Sarah Sue. "Yes. I think I'd like that. I enjoyed helping Brady and then Samson. With the house almost empty, it would be nice to have more four-legged companions. Especially when Kade and Cassie move and take Brady with them."

"Good." Sarah Sue patted her mother-in-law's hand. "I was hoping you'd say that. There isn't the flow of dogs there had been after Afghanistan, but there are still too many service dogs needing training before they can live a retired life with a nice family."

"I'm in." Alice blushed. "I mean, we're in."

And that said it all for Josh. There definitely had to be something in the water on this ranch. Love, trust, communication, touch, and joy. Yep. Definitely the water.

Clint pushed to his feet. "I'm going to grab a beer. Anyone want something?" His gaze drifted from person to person at the table.

When his eyes met Josh's, he heard himself say, "I'll have a glass of water."

Enjoy an excerpt from
Sweet Rescue

Josh Coleman tightened the chin strap on his tactical helmet and checked his vest seals. Sweat slid down his spine, but his focus stayed locked on the six-vehicle convoy lined up for inspection.

"Transport three's thermal reading is climbing faster than the others." Scanning the line, he clipped the handheld scanner to his tactical vest. Responsible for convoy security, these routine checks had become second nature during his years of service.

Kade Sweet, his longtime friend and the Military Working Dog handler assigned to their team, approached with Rambo, the Belgian Malinois, trotting attentively at his side. Fitted to his muscular frame, the dog's tactical vest matched their own. "All set?"

"Right about now, I'd kill for some of your mother's strawberry lemonade."

"Tell me about it." Kade chuckled. No doubt his buddy's thoughts were taking a detour to the Sweet family ranch, quiet evenings, soft breezes, and his mother's lemonade. A quick blink and he was all business again. "Rambo already cleared the first two vehicles. No alerts for explosives. What's the issue with transport three?"

"Looks like a coolant leak." Josh gestured toward the heavy truck carrying fuel reserves for the joint training exercise. "I'm not taking chances with that much combustible material on board."

As convoy security commander for this mission, Josh had final say on safety protocols. The chain of command was clear—he made the decisions, his team executed them, and everyone got home safe. The straightforward nature of this assignment should have made it routine: escort training ordnance and fuel supplies to the far range where a joint exercise was scheduled to begin tomorrow morning. Simple enough on paper.

The transport driver approached, wiping sweat from his brow. "Problem, Staff Sergeant?"

"Need to check your engine compartment." Josh's tone was professional but left no room for debate. "Pop the hood."

The driver complied, releasing the hood latch with a metallic click. Josh leaned in carefully, avoiding the scorching metal components. His training had taught him to trust his instincts, and something about this situation felt off. A small puddle of green liquid had formed beneath the radiator, and the coolant reservoir showed a hairline crack along one side.

"Losing coolant fast," Josh stepped back. "This vehicle isn't going anywhere until it's replaced." He turned to Specialist Boglioli, his communications operator. "Radio base. We need a replacement transport before we continue the mission."

"But we're already behind schedule," the driver protested. "Can't we just add more coolant and keep an eye on it?"

Josh fixed the driver with a steady gaze. "Not with what you're hauling. One spark near a fuel leak and this whole convoy lights up like the Fourth of July."

Moving closer, Kade kept Rambo on a short lead. "Listen to the man," his easy Texas drawl masked the authority in his voice. "Staff Sergeant Coleman's been running convoy security since before you could shave."

The driver's shoulders stiffened under the rebuke. "Yes, Staff Sergeant."

Josh nodded to Kade as the driver walked away. "Thanks for the backup."

"No problem." Kade crouched to check Rambo's tactical vest, adjusting a strap that had loosened. "Dog's been acting antsy since we stopped. He's flagging something."

Scanning the sparse landscape around them, Josh frowned. Training grounds stretched for miles in every direction, mostly scrubby terrain broken by the occasional patch of mesquite trees and dirt roads. Nothing but heat waves shimmered on the horizon. "Think the heat's getting to Rambo?"

Kade shook his head. "He's desert-trained. This is nothing for him." He gave a quick hand signal toward the front of the line. Rambo trotting beside him, he called over his shoulder, "I'll finish clearing the lead trucks."

Josh waved acknowledgment, turning his attention back to the idling transports. They hadn't gone ten yards when Rambo suddenly stopped mid-stride, muscles going rigid, his head snapping back toward the rear of the convoy. A low growl rumbled from deep in his chest, sharp and warning.

Frozen in place, Kade's hand hovered near his sidearm. "What is it, boy?" He followed the dog's focus toward the fuel trucks behind them.

Josh's pulse spiked. Rambo wasn't one to false-alert—something back there wasn't right.

The radio on Josh's shoulder crackled to life followed by Boglioli's raspy voice. "Base confirms replacement transport ETA forty minutes, Staff Sergean."

"Roger that," Josh's attention remained fixed on Rambo's behavior. By detecting threats before human senses could, military working dogs had saved their lives more than once during previous deployments. Josh would trust a well-trained K9 before humans any day of the week. Something sharp and chemical tainted the air—too faint for his nose, but dogs didn't false-flag.

"Check the rear vehicles again. Full inspection."

"On it," Kade nodded, already moving with Rambo toward the back of the convoy.

Josh followed, signaling for two more team members to join them. If Rambo sensed something wrong, there was a reason. Whatever was wrong up front wasn't what had Rambo spooked. Different truck, different threat.

They approached the rear transport—another fuel truck—where Rambo's behavior intensified. The dog strained against his lead, hackles raised, growling more loudly now.

"Something's definitely got him worked up," Kade's voice dropped to a near whisper as he maintained control of his partner.

Josh gestured for the driver to step away from the vehicle. "When's the last time you checked your engine temperature?"

"Just before we left base, Staff Sergeant. Everything was normal."

About to take a reading, Josh reached for his scanner when a sharp metallic crack echoed from somewhere beneath the truck. The sound wasn't loud—barely audible over the idling engines—but Josh's combat-honed instincts registered it instantly. It wasn't a mechanical pop; that hollow metallic snap had the signature of something man-made under tension, about to give. Adrenaline shot through his system. "Clear the area!" Moving at full speed, he waved his arms, directing his team to a safe distance. "Everybody back now!"

The world seemed to turn in slow motion. Josh sprinted toward the front of the convoy, shouting orders as he moved. "Boglioli! Get the lead vehicles moving!"

Having just finished checking the forward vehicles, Kade and Rambo were again at the front of the convoy. Josh could see him turning at the commotion.

"Possible detonation! Clear out!" Josh bellowed, urging nearby soldiers to move faster. Two men were still too close to the suspect vehicle, frozen in momentary confusion. Damn it. He changed direction, rushing toward them. "Move!" Josh shoved the nearest soldier forward.

The blast hit before he cleared the path, followed instantly by another detonation. The shockwave caught Josh and the two soldiers in the open, lifting them off their feet. He felt himself hurled through the air, a blinding flash searing his vision as the pounding force crushed against his chest, slamming him to the ground. Beside him one soldier wasn't moving, the other lay several feet away, unnaturally still. His chest burned, his side screamed.

Through the ringing in his ears, he caught a flash of Kade dragging Rambo behind the lead truck—both safe. Relief flickered, even as darkness closed in.

His only clear thought—what an unholy mess.

Thumbing through the last pages of her mystery novel, Katie Lawford confirmed her guess halfway through the book had been accurate. No point in finishing it now. One week into the government shutdown, and she'd already cleaned out her closet, labeled her spice jars, put dividers in her junk drawer, binged two seasons of a show she'd been meaning to watch for ages, and finished three books from her "to-be-read" pile.

She glanced at her phone. No alerts, no panicked emails from her supervisor, no updates about when the Department of Defense contract administrators might return to work. Just silence and the ticking of her grandmother's antique clock. "So much for those *urgent* military supply contracts," she muttered, stretching her legs on the couch. The unexpected furlough had been nice—at first. But now, a week later, restlessness was settling in.

Her phone buzzed. *Finally.* She snatched it up. "You rescued me from organizing the freezer."

Jackie Sweet's laugh came through bright and familiar. "Tell me you're not still cleaning. It's a furlough, not a punishment."

"It's both." Katie dropped onto the sofa. "I've rearranged every shelf I own. Even the ones that don't need rearranging."

"We can't have that." There was a long pause. "So, tell me. How are you doing really? I mean. Do you need money or something?"

Oh how she loved her bestie. She couldn't help but smile. "I'm fine. I have a very understanding landlady. Mrs.

O'Grady has been through this before. Whenever the government shuts down, lots of Houston contractors wind up home sitting on their hands with no paychecks. She knows we'll get paid eventually, so she's told me it's all right to hold off on rent until I get a paycheck. Even though I have a good nest egg just in case."

"Well, that's a start."

Another long pause and Katie knew Jackie was stewing on something. "Might as well spit it out."

"Why don't you come ride this shut down out here? It's been ages and we'd all love to have you."

"Oh, sure. You and Garrett are still technically newlyweds. I bet he wants a fifth wheel tagging along about as much as he wants to step on a rusty nail—barefoot."

"Don't be silly. Garrett loves having you around as much as I do."

"Uh huh."

"Really."

"Right."

"Come on. You know what this house is like. Organized chaos with a double dose of love and laughter."

Her friend had a point. She'd only spent a few days at the ranch for Jackie and Garrett's wedding, and there was never a moment when anyone was alone, and that seemed just fine with everyone. Heck, half the siblings were still living at the house and they were all newlyweds.

"Carson and Jess' house is really taking shape. They put the sheetrock up this last week and it's actually looking like a house and not so much like a kid's construction toy."

"I bet they can hardly wait." She remembered the talk about starting building as soon as some of the family business was taken care of. Mason their son was the most excited about having his own house while torn about leaving his Nonnie alone in the Main house. It was kind of cute.

"Now if you want to be helpful, the guest annex is down to the cosmetic stages. Alice picked out the paint colors the other day. Mostly soft beiges and yellows."

"Yellow?" She couldn't picture Alice Sweet picking out

yellows for that big old western style home.

"I think she calls it warm butter." Jackie chuckled. "The funny thing, she looked at a something ivory for the bathroom and to me that thing looked like French mustard. No idea where these companies get their color names from."

"You don't want my opinion. Last time I helped you paint your living room wall looked like a bad Picasso."

"That's only because you grabbed the wrong paint can."

"It said living room."

"And here we go again. *Trim*. It said living room trim." Jackie's laughter now was a far cry from the horror on her face when she walked into the room and found her camel walls blotched with patches of not quite white over every filled nail hole.

"A very valid reason why I should never be given a paint brush."

"Okay. No painting," Jackie's voice still held a healthy dose of humor. "But seriously, when's the last time you had a vacation? And I don't mean time off to clean out your closet or catch up on your laundry. A real get out of town vacation?"

"I get out of town."

"I don't mean for weddings."

Well that poked a hole in her argument. "Touché."

"Does that mean you'll come out and visit?"

"What if congress stops the pissing match and we all have to go back to work?"

"Then you go home, but when have you ever known a shutdown to last only a week?"

Point to Jackie. "Let me think about it."

"Don't think. Pack."

Had her friend always been this pushy? Her mind turned to when Jackie gave up everything to chase after the wrong man. Yep, she'd always been this pushy. "I'll think about it."

"Well," Jackie sighed. "I guess I'll have to settle for that. For now."

Setting her phone on the side table, Katie looked around. She really did love her little garage apartment.

Nestled in the Memorial neighborhood of downtown Houston, there were mature trees lining every street, lots of colorful blooms, well manicured lawns, and no cookie cutter homes—yet. This apartment had lots of character, and she liked that. Her gaze landed on her dwindling pile of books to read. It was time to face facts; she was bored out of her mind, but West Texas?

Once more she took in her surroundings. Before she realized what she was doing, she found herself in her room, yanking her suitcase out of the closet. "West Texas here I come."

Sweet Rescue is available now

MEET CHRIS

USA TODAY Bestselling Author of dozens of contemporary novels, including the award winning Aloha Series, Chris Keniston lives in suburban Dallas with her husband, two human children, and two canine children. Though she loves her puppies equally, she admits being especially attached to her German Shepherd rescue. After all, even dogs deserve a happily ever after.

More on Chris and all her books can be found at
www.chriskeniston.com

Follow Chris' Monday Blog at her website
ChrisKenistonAuthor

Follow Chris on Facebook at
ChrisKenistonAuthor

Never miss a New Release!
Sign up for News from Chris:
www.chriskeniston.com/newsletter.html

Questions? Comments?
I would love to hear from you! You can reach me at:
chris@chriskeniston.com